THE NEWS WAS OUT.

All over town.

The 504th might never again fly a single mission, perhaps not even a training flight. But in just nine hours, it was already beginning to look like an aviation unit of the United States Army.

There was this green-eyed, left-handed, Indian looking eagle colonel, who had come down on this cruddy 504 outfit like a ton of chickenshit off a twenty-story building. And it was getting all over everyone in sight, and it looked like it was only going to get worse. Hell, they might even have to start flying missions again!

To the men Brown said, "The resemblance is vague, but clearly discernible. I think you people have returned from whatever filthy, rotten place you've been and come back into the army."

Joe Brown looked at his watch. It was 0025 hours—twenty-five minutes past midnight. "Breakfast at zero five hundred hours. Sleep fast, men; it'll be here soon."

As he passed out through the corridor down between the rows of benches, Brown heard some unknown voice say, "Goddamn, it doesn't take long to spend a night with that son of a bitch, does it?"

GUNSHIP COMMANDER

by
William Crawford

PINNACLE BOOKS • NEW YORK CITY

This book is for W. C. Crawford—my uncle—and
Mildred II.

GUNSHIP COMMANDER

Copyright © 1973 by Lyle Kenyon Engel

Produced by Lyle Kenyon Engel

A Pinnacle Books original edition, published for the first time
anywhere.

First printing, October 1973

Printed in the United States of America

PINNACLE BOOKS, INC.
275 Madison Avenue
New York, N.Y. 10016

AUTHOR'S NOTE

To the author's knowledge there is not now and there never has been a unit in United States Army Aviation designated the 504th. This book is a novel; it is entirely fiction; if the names of any real people, alive or dead, appear in this novel, it is purely coincidental.

The author wishes to express his gratitude to Mr. Larry M. Hayes and Mr. Frank Topping of the Bell Helicopter Company; to former Lt. JPSB & J; to Colonel REL; to DLW; to FLF; and as always to KBC.

5

1

The man stood on a hilltop and looked down through the trees at the small Arizona town. He was dressed in heavy underwear, thick socks and racers, a pair of sweat pants and a hooded sweat shirt. The man looked younger than he was. Every morning he took this early-morning run, a mile out through the mountain forest and a mile and a half back, the longer distance on the return, because he circled through town to go by the post office and pick up his mail. He was a tall man, lean and long-muscled more than big, except across the chest and shoulders. When the man moved every movement was controlled, lithe, easy gliding motions, like a boxer might make; and this was no accident. During three years in college he captained the boxing team and was NCAA light-heavyweight champion, and the following year, all-Army champion in the same weight class.

The man's skin was dark and there was an Indian slant to his eyes; the eyes were the color of ripe green limes. He breathed deeply three times, jogged down the hill, along a road spread with reddish-colored gravel, breathing deeply of the cold, smoke-scented air. He stopped before the tiny building and went through the door under the sign:

UNITED STATES POST OFFICE
Pinetop, Arizona 85935

The clerk behind the counter looked up and grinned, lifted a hand in greeting and said, "Morning, Joe! Been for your run?"

"Every day, pard," the man answered, as he walked over to his box, opened it and took out the mail, including a fat envelope he had been expecting for more than a

7

week. With the certainty of knowing what message the envelope contained he hardly looked at it, except to verify that it was, indeed, his:

LT COL Joseph Paul Brown, USA
P.O. Box 552
Pinetop, Arizona 85935

Joe Brown waved again to the clerk behind the counter and went out the door. He jogged up the graveled road, turned off on a steep two-lane track, circled around and entered the back gate of a large fenced lot, more than an acre, that had a two-story house, a small barn, and what Joe Brown called his "camp." It was a small, steeply roofed building, about ten feet wide and twice as long. He opened the door, went inside and sat down at the old captain's chair before his desk. On the wall were photos of himself. If you looked at them closely, you could trace Joe Brown's career; from West Point cadet and NCAA champion boxer, in the late nineteen-forties, through graduation from aviation flight school at Fort Hood, Texas; combat in Korea and Cold War assignments; and that he had, somehow, become personally acquainted with some extremely well-known people—film stars, politicians, several astronauts, a President of the United States and a number of newsmen.

Brown plugged in an electric heater to warm the room a bit before he stripped off his sweat shirt and loosened the waist-string of his sweat pants. He shoved the fat, official letter aside and went through the rest of the mail. An amusing postcard, from a crazy cowpuncher in Texas who had ridden too many bucking horses and so addled his brain that he was now trying to become a writer. The telephone and electric bills. A note from a colleague in Vietnam that Brown read with care, reread parts of, shaking his head and thinking, "God, how glad I am to be done with that crappy little, rotten war!"

He glanced over at one photo in a black frame on the wall. It was not a photograph that would inflate Joe Brown's ego to any marked degree. It showed him on the floor of a boxing ring, face twisted in pain, his stomach

8

muscles knotted and the cords of his neck standing out like cables as he reached for the bottom rope, trying to climb back to his feet. He never made it, and he never fought again, seriously, after that. What did not show in the picture was Joe Brown's left hand. In the photograph, the left hand looked like any other hand laced inside a boxing glove. The part which did not show was where the hand was broken in three places. Those three breaks made a total of seventeen times that he'd broken bones in that hand and it convinced him that a professional military career, for which he was trained, was superior to that of a professional prize fighter, for which he was also trained but did not have good hands for.

Looking at that picture made Joe Brown decide, once more, that he had done the right thing, in spite of Vietnam. Once more, he read over part of the letter from his friend, then, put it aside and picked up the fat, official envelope.

He slit it with an old M-1 carbine bayonet, souvenir from Korea. He took out the sheaf of more than a dozen copies of what he knew were his orders; the papers that would tell him when and where to report after his leave ended and the job assignment he would have.

He skipped down through the military jargon and found the name of the duty station. At first, it simply did not register; it did not register because it did not make sense; it did not make sense simply because it must be a mistake.

Brown folded the creases in the paper backwards, smoothed out the papers on his desk and stared at them. He could not believe what he read. He even looked back to the top of the page to make sure it had his name on it and that these were not some other officer's orders put into the wrong envelope.

When he read it the third time and realized it was true the pain hit him. Had Joe Brown not known better, he would have believed he was having a heart attack; that's how much it hurt. The pain in his chest area was like broken glass, with a tight band around his body, cinching

9

down. He made it to the door before he started throwing up. That is how his wife, Jody, found him, bent over and vomiting, holding on to the doorsill of his camp with one brown hand.

2

Colonel Joe Brown's voice was a flat, level crackling of words, like a train running fast across switches when he said, "You're god damn right I know to *whom* I am talking! General, sir, Pate Randolph, and I am requesting, *sir,* that you either go yourself or send some lard assed aide over there to give that computer a kick in the ass! And see if you can get my name unstuck inside the son of a bitch."

Brown listened for a moment, knuckles white as he gripped the telephone, and then he spoke again, his voice pitched lower, but the edge of fury even more cutting. "I have already spent four miserable, rotten years of my life in that shit-hole and I am not going back. Goddamn it, we are pulling out over there. Haven't you heard? It's been in all the papers."

". . . All right, sir, I apologize for the sarcasm." Brown listened a moment longer, then: "Yes, sir, I will. Tonight at ten, your time. Yes, sir, I have the number. Goodbye, sir."

Brown put down the telephone and turned to his wife. For a moment they simply stood and looked at one another, ten feet apart, but a space that neither seemed able to cross and close, until they both moved at once. He held her and felt her shudder. Jody always cried that way, inside, without sound. You could look at her and unless you knew her well enough to detect the signs, you could not tell she was going to pieces, inside. She had been this way for the better part of three hours, since Joe had come roaring into the house with such violence he unhinged the back door, and kicked a chair to splinters fit only for fireplace kindling as he made for the telephone. He had

11

said nothing to her, only handed her the orders as he picked up the telephone and, with the greatest effort of will, made himself talk quietly and courteously to all the operators and in-between-people, until he got General Randolph on the line.

Then the whole house seemed to shake.

And it had not done one damned bit of good.

Pate Randolph, because of personal friendship—he had been Joe's boxing coach at the Point—let him get by with a lot of shouting and too much cursing. He had let him off the hook by telling him he had another long distance call, and that Brown should cool off and call back that evening at Pate's home in Fort Myer, and they could work it out, surely. . . .

As he held his wife in his arms, Brown felt another stabbing ulcer attack coming on and he had to release her and make it to the toilet. Dry heaves. He'd lost all his breakfast in the sour upgush earlier. He got half-and-half milk from the refrigerator, a bottle of white, chalky pills from the dresser-top, and the little green-and-black ones that made his pain something he could live with, after another ten minutes of agony.

As he lay back in the big chair before the fireplace and let the medication work, Jody came and sat on the floor beside him. She put the side of her face on his hard muscular thigh. "Joe? . . ."

"Yes, honey?"

"You're going, aren't you?"

"No."

"Joe. . . ."

"I'm not going. I'll resign my commission. I won't go back. They can shove it."

"You don't mean that."

"You watch how I mean it, love."

"They won't let you do it."

"They can't stop me."

"You know better than that."

"What the hell can they do? I resign, that's all. I sign some god damn papers. They hand me a paper, and I'm

12

out. I lose my pension. I have to pay for fixing my own teeth. I bust up that jangly hand in a bar fight and pay the doctor from my own pocket. No more PX discounts. I get a job. What the hell—?"

"They won't let go that easily, that simply."

"What do you mean?"

"I mean that picture on the wall out there in your camp. The one of you and the president. They won't let you go, Joe, just like that."

"They can't stop me."

"They can stop you, or send you to jail."

Brown came up fast, so fast he had to catch his wife's shoulders to keep her from falling. She looked up at him and he knew she was crying again, without a sound.

He waited it out, unable to help her, and finally she managed to say, "They won't let you decide for yourself that you will not return to Vietnam for the fifth time. To avoid doing so resign your commission, and they will issue a direct order. General Pate Randolph will fly to Phoenix and have a helicopter drop him in our backyard and personally issue that order, if necessary. Then it won't be a matter of resigning, Joe. It will be direct disobedience, and so flagrant that some of the media will call you a traitor, and the others try to make a leftist folk hero of you."

"God damn, kid, you've really thought it out, haven't you?"

She nodded.

He reached down and put his finger under her chin, so he could look into her brown eyes. "Jody, have you forgotten why we are married?"

She shook her head.

"I don't think you understand what I mean."

"Because we love each other?"

Joe nodded. "That's right. We love one another. I never knew there could be anything so rich and pure and *good* as our love." Then his voice became as hard and ruthless as a bayonet thrust through the guts. "But we'd never have had the chance, never had that first date, that

13

first touch, if Ken Engel had not died in a shit-filled ditch out there in that worthless, sorry country and its rotten little war. Doing his *fourth* god damn tour of duty, and for what? For Christ's sake, Jody! . . . No! Absolutely not. I won't go out again. You've been a widow once."

Jody got to her feet and came to him, kissed him, then turned and went toward the kitchen, murmuring just loud enough so Colonel Brown heard. "You'll go, Joe-Paul. You don't know how *not* to do your job. You've never had any practice."

To himself, Joe Brown thought, I will ground myself. They can't make a man with ulcers fly; it's a potential hazard, a known disability, as they say in their god damn rule books. And that is what he told General Pate Randolph when he called that evening.

Randolph laughed at him. "Joe, you were, and are, obviously so up to your ass in alligators over returning to Southeast Asia, you failed to read everything in that envelope. You're no longer a light colonel, but one with the eagle. Command function. You have no flying assignment."

"And that's supposed to be doing me some kind of big favor, is it, General? You know, as well as I do, that getting into aviation had as much to do with my staying in the army, as a career, as did my worthless left hand."

"They will be your helicopters, Colonel. Who flies them is strictly your business. Unless, of course, you ground yourself because of ulcers."

"What's the outfit?"

"I, ah, well, that information will be given to you upon reporting in."

"If I go."

The general's voice got iron-hard. "The game is over, Colonel Brown. Make up your mind. On the date stated in your orders, you either report to United States Army Headquarters for Aviation, Southeast Asia; or you report to me in my office."

"To hear charges and specifications, I suppose."

"Precisely."

14

"It's a wonderful thing to be a good horse. The best part is how bastards like you absolutely *insist* on working them to death."

"Now, Joe, I know how you must feel, but—"

"Fuck you, General Randolph! Sir."

3

If anything had changed in Southeast Asia since Colonel Joe Brown departed *Ton Son Nhut* airport seven months earlier, he could not tell what it was. Everything still stank of shit and blood and corruption, graft and intrigue, stinking feet and rotten armpits; and the flickering hatred behind the dark eyes in the bland faces.

The taxi that carried him to town was a deathtrap and the driver, a crazed, plump young man had missed his true calling in life having been born too late and in the wrong country: he was an outstanding recruit for Japan's *kamikaze* squadron. When he stopped before headquarters and Joe got out the driver demanded twice the agreed-upon fare, and, since a Viet cop stood nearby, the driver kept raising his voice and making wide, then wider, gestures.

For a moment Colonel Joe Brown simply looked at the driver. Then he told him in fluent and almost flawless Vietnamese, learned in four one-year-tours of duty, "Get out of here before I cave your flat face in."

The cop, who had started over to see what the problem was, and, perhaps to slice off a little of the overcharge for himself, made an abrupt precise aboutface and marched smartly back to his post.

Brown hired two porters to carry his gear up into headquarters and told them where to put it in the transient officers waiting room and lounge. He paid the men, bought a soft drink from the coin-operated machine, took three of the chalky pills, smoked half a cigarette, and felt about as ready as he'd get. He went into the arrival office and handed over his orders.

16

Brown was not surprised at his reception. The young enlisted man who took the papers read the name and his eyes got wide. He excused himself and hustled over to a desk and gave the orders to a Negro second lieutenant, who shot to his feet, came across the room in six long strides and said, "Please, sir, Colonel Brown, if you will, follow me. Colonel March is expecting you."

"I'll just bet he is."

"I beg your pardon, sir?"

"Never mind."

Colonel March was a big man, running to fat. He came from behind his desk like an appliance salesman, hand out, all white teeth and crinkling blue eyes; sun-lamp-dark tan. He dismissed the lieutenant and gestured toward a chair, "Joe, sit down. It's been a long time."

"Yeah, five months."

"Well, not so long, I suppose. Rotten luck, too. Still putting pennies in the jar, weren't you?"

"If you mean I was still on my honeymoon, yes. Jody and I got married two months ago, tomorrow."

"Rotten luck."

"I think you said that once."

"Hell, Joe, don't be sore at *me*. I didn't—"

"What have you got for me?" Joe Brown did not like the way March's eyes slid off to look past Brown's shoulder when he asked March that question. It was the look of a man ready, but perhaps unwilling, to tell a lie. March said, "Joe, have you had any lunch?"

Joe Brown did not say anything. He looked steadily at March and the colonel behind the desk could not maintain eye contact. Joe Brown thought, I would not want to buy anything used off this creep, a freezer or washing machine with a thirty-day guarantee.

March said, "How about it, Joe? Some lunch? After the flight, a long tall cold one will do you good."

"I can't drink. I've got a bleeding ulcer."

"Gee, Joe, that's tough news. I hope—"

"Are you about through?"

17

"Through, Joe?"

"With the pitch. What are you setting me up for, March? What are you trying to sell me?"

"You Point guys—"

"Now don't get your poor little *Texas A & M* hiny in an inferiority-complex-uproar, Colonel March. You're just as good as us white guys."

"All right, since you can't even accept normal—"

"You've been out here too long, Colonel. You're getting like the French and the Viets and all the other spooks everywhere we go. You're getting a real feel for ritual, all the little niceties before handing over the bag of shit."

"And you've been somewhere else too long. It is not necessary to talk like a common soldier."

"If I bring a note from my mother, can I be excused?"

"God Almighty, Joe!" March leaped to his feet, "What in God's name is *wrong* with you?"

"I am so god damn sore, so mad, so pissed off, so round the bend with anger, I can hardly keep from bursting into tears."

"Why savage me?"

"You're handy, and you are about to hand me something that stinks, something you took out from under a rotten old board."

"What the hell can I do? I'm just the guy who has the job of telling you."

"Not quite. I know you, March. You're strong. You're ambitious, you've got connections, know all the right people. Why you even screwed—what's her name, the one with the big tits?—the last time she came out to *USO* the troops."

"What do you want from me, for Christ's sake?"

"An office right here in this building. Handle the mail. See all the toilets are kept clean. I'll tend bar at the officer's club. I don't want whatever you've got ready for me. I've had mine, four times."

"I never thought I'd ever, *ever* hear Joe Brown say things like that."

"That I'm scared, a coward?"

"Y—" March had a lot of trouble getting it out, because Brown saw that March was not sure, quite, that fear was what Joe Brown was talking about.

"I'm always scared, and so are you, and everyone else who's got any sense. But I'm not a coward. I'm not afraid of going where you want to send me, and I'll go . . . just as soon as you, or your boss, or that frigging Randolph, or the President himself gives a *reason* for going."

March simply stared. The longer he stared, the wider his eyes got, and, finally, he laughed, not loud, and shook his head. After a moment he looked up again and Brown heard the words that a man like March had to say, because he was a man like March. "Joe, this is the *army*. You're a career army *officer*. My God, man, you're talking like some of these punk enlisted men we've got, their hair tied back with a beaded headband, stoned on marijuana and plotting how to frag an officer they don't like."

Brown knew he couldn't have touched March with a sixty-foot insulated pole. It was useless to try. He said, "I want to talk to your boss."

"General Paulson's not in today."

"Not in, or not in for Joe Brown?"

"Joe, let me be as candid as you insist on being. You've got your ass clear up over your shoulders, and you don't even know why. You don't even know what your assignment *is!*"

"I don't have to know when Randolph refuses to tell me, and when I ask you, you invite me to lunch. When I boxed, it was my *hand* that got busted up seventeen times, not my brains. A child could figure it out. What you've got me set up for is something bad, March; it's something so bad you can't talk about it without choking. Just cut the crap and let's have it."

March took a deep breath, staring at Brown, but Joe saw that when March began to speak, he could not keep his chin up. He looked down at his hands. "It's the Five-Oh-Fourth, Joe."

The words so numbed Joe Brown that he hardly felt the stomach-full-of-broken-glass-splinters pain of his ulcer hit him. He just sat there, like a man with all his strings cut and his bones turned to smoke. He knew it had to be something bad; he never thought it would be the worst possible.

March started to say something: "Joe, I—"

Brown said, "If you tell me you're sorry, I swear to Christ I'll punch every tooth out of your mealy god damn mouth."

March nodded. He reached across the desk in silence, endorsed Brown's orders and shoved them back. In a dull and almost toneless voice, March said, "Your transportation to the airport is ready, waiting down front. A helicopter from your command is at *Ton Son Nhut*. Good luck."

March did not get to his feet; he did not offer to shake hands. Probably he was afraid Joe Brown would hit him, and he'd had to bribe the army dentist at Huntsville with five cases of whiskey to put on those beautiful, white caps.

Brown found a couple of Viets loafing around the hallways and ordered them to carry his gear down to the waiting jeep. The driver asked, "Colonel Brown?" as he got out and saluted. Joe nodded as he returned the salute and climbed into the jeep. Neither of them said another word until the driver pulled to a stop beside a helicopter at the airport.

Brown could not believe it. He had heard all the tales, all the stories, read the story in *Time* and seen the pictures on television, but he still could not believe it.

The driver unloaded Brown's gear and climbed back into the jeep, anxious. Brown got out and stood, just looking. Probably it was a helicopter. What it looked like was a pile of junk with the vague lines of a helicopter; one of those mobiles that are fashionable back in the States. They hang from strings or wires, made of old

20

pieces of tin can, welding rod, copper wire, clothespin springs; junk.

Three men lay in the shade under the helicopter; they looked like shaggy thugs, Bowery bums, or like what people call *hippies*, nowadays. They did not move. After a long stare, one of the men turned his head and spat a long stream of brown tobacco juice. He turned his face back to Brown and wiped his grinning lips.

Another man, wearing pilot's gear, with a faded white stripe sewed on his collar tab leaned against the fuselage with his arms folded. He did not move. He stared steadily and without blinking with intense blue eyes, straight into Brown's eyes. Another man squatted in the side hatch beside the gunmount, also in pilot dress, a newer-looking warrant-officer's cloth bar sewed to his collar tab.

For more than a minute, the scene remained without motion or sound. Brown went to the smallest of his gear and from an old, stained musette bag, he took a .45 caliber Colt automatic pistol. He shoved it into his waistband just above his left hip, then took off the summer-weight blouse he wore and his necktie. He folded the clothing atop his largest duffel bag. He took a clean white handkerchief from his hip pocket and wrapped it around his left hand. Binding it tightly and using his teeth and right hand, he knotted it into place.

As Brown did these various maneuvers, the men began to stir; and stare. The three prone men under the helicopter sat up; old Spitter crawled from under the ship as though he needed a better view. Brown walked directly to the aircraft commander, the first lieutenant with the white tab. Brown stopped very close to the man, too close; so close the 1/Lt. straightened up from his slouch and pressed himself back against the fuselage. But he assumed nothing approaching the position of attention and there was a snotty, smirky smile twisting his lips.

Brown said to the man, "Report."

The man mumbled something that sounded rather like

21

"Lieutenant Dale Walker." He did not say, "Sir," and he did not salute.

Brown said, "Report properly."

Walker came more or less to the position of attention, waved his right hand in the vicinity of his forehead, and mumbled his name again, neglecting to add, "sir."

"You have one more opportunity," Brown said in a deadly level, calm voice.

Walker grinned and looked over his shoulder at the copilot and, then, at Spitter, who'd edged closer and had a wild, eager stare in his eyes. The other two men began crawling from under the aircraft.

"Hey, Skipper," old Spitter said, "looks like our new chicken colonel is chicken clear through, shit'n' all."

All the men laughed.

Then Walker raised both hands and shoved Brown's shoulders, saying with a raw edge of hatred in his voice, "Don't stand so close, buster. You're crowding."

Brown got him with the best low-left-hook he had, and the punch caught Walker just where Brown aimed, for the liver. Walker made a noise like a man dying of saw blades through the guts and fell unconscious on the concrete ramp beside the helicopter. By this time Brown had turned, blocked Spitter's wild haymaking right hand, slipped inside, drove a knee into Spitter's groin, kicked him in the head going down and heard Spitter's jaw crack.

Brown stepped back and put his hands on his hips, but his left hand did not touch the pistol in his waistband. To one of the other men who'd been lying under the ship, Brown said, "Roll him over before he chokes on that mouthful of tobacco."

The man leaped to obey.

Brown looked up at the copilot. "Your turn now, sonny."

The copilot jumped to the ground. He came to rigid attention. He grooved a precise salute and in exact military parlance, with proper respect in his tone of voice, he reported: "Warrant Officer Walter John Bass, sir." After

22

he ceased speaking, his mouth kept working, lips moving over and under.

Brown could not resist saying, "It figures."

"Sir? . . ."

"Never mind. Can you fly this pile of junk?"

"Yes, sir!"

"Then get my gear aboard, load these two shits," Brown pointed at Walker and Spitter, "and let's go. I'm not current, so you sit in the right seat."

Upon landing at the 504th's base, Brown was not surprised to see that it looked more like photographs he had seen of a commune than it did a military establishment. He told Warrant Bass, "Get military policemen to take charge of those two." Brown pointed to the now barely conscious Walker, and the sobbing, face-holding Spitter. Brown turned to one of the other men. "Find the adjutant and have him report to me at once."

The man saluted and took off in a run. From the sides of his eyes Brown looked at the men who had started to gather around for a look at the "new broom." All were dirty and ragged. Some wore necklaces with peace signs, and a few had hair so long it was tied back in a horsetail. Many of them openly grinned and spat, or crouched in available shade and made displays of fondling fragmentation grenades or weapons. Brown stood in the sun and waited, hands on hips, but not touching the .45 Colt.

The adjutant arrived first, a fat man, puffing, red in the face, the burst veins of a heavy steady boozer on his beaked nose. He saluted sloppily, and said his name was Captain Andy King. He needed a shave and kept trying to tuck in his shirttail.

"King, prepare charges and specifications against these two men." Brown jerked a thumb at Walker and Spitter, "and lock them up together after you get that one's jaw wired together."

"But, sir, he is an enlisted man."

"Who the hell is *he*?"

"That man there, sir, Charles. Sergeant Travis Charles."

"That's all right, Captain King, put them in together. They seem to be crazy about one another, real buddies."

"Sir— Ah, what are the charges?"

"Physical assault upon a superior officer."

"Sir— If I may ask . . . whom did they assault?"

"Me." Brown grinned. "It was bad judgment, wouldn't you say?"

"Very much so," King said, his veined eyes wide with wonder.

The MPs came up, just a bit enough neater than the others in view so that Brown immediately had some respect for the military police commander in the 504 area. They loaded Walker and Charles into their jeep and drove away to the hospital as Brown ordered King to call all the unit's officers together and have someone bring his gear.

Then Brown turned to the men who'd gathered around, and to the one man who had made such a display of fondling a frag grenade while he squatted on the ground, Brown pointed and said, "You fuckfaced animal. Either do something with that or put it away. And if I ever see you with it again, I'll blow your god damned cruddy head off." He started toward the man, who fell backwards and then scrambled sideways like a crab, in his desperation to get away. Brown picked up the grenade, looked at it, threw it hard and fast with the three-quarter motion of a lefthanded fast-ball pitcher. The grenade struck the chest of another of the displayers, who'd made a big production of sliding back and forth the action of his Type 50 MAT 49 submachine gun, a favorite weapon of the Viet Cong.

"Where did you get it?" Brown asked the man, who now lay in the dust holding himself. "Buy it off an infantryman? Steal it from some fighting man?"

Brown walked over and picked up the MAT, took out the clip, hurled it as far as he could, jammed the gun muzzle down in the dirt and walked away.

Behind him there was complete, utter silence.

Brown knew better than to think the silence arose from

respect or even from awe; it was the silence of hatred. It had a feel and a stink to it, as well as the absence of sound.

It was almost the same kind of silence that greeted him twenty minutes later at officers' call.

4

Brown stood on a platform in the briefing room; it looked just like the platforms and the briefing rooms he'd seen in a hundred war movies before he ever sat down inside a similar room himself. With some kind of astonishment, he realized that his ulcer did not hurt; he did not feel as if there were a dagger buried in him just below the breastbone. And, he acknowledged silently and to himself, he felt just slightly like an ass. All he could see down the tunnel of his mind for a moment was Gregory Peck in *Twelve O'Clock High.*

He wasn't Gregory Peck if for no other reason than because Joe Brown's eyes were green and he was left-handed; but, mainly, because this was not a war they were fighting to win but just fighting.

That was the trouble; that was the problem. Joe Brown felt exactly the same way about this whole miserable mess, this shit-hole country, the graft and corruption, the politicking, the fashionable mouthings from both hawks and doves, the whole rotten stinking pile of crap—he felt about it precisely as did the men who sat on crude wooden benches out there in front of him, hating him.

But the crunch had come to him.

Not here. Not in Saigon. Not at the airport when he savaged the pilot and the sergeant.

The crunch came in a lovely home, that was for a short, too-short while, a honeymoon cottage in the mountains in Arizona.

"*You don't know how* not *to do your job, Joe Brown. You've never had any practice.*"

It was time to go to work. After creaming Walker and

cracking Charles' jaw and threatening the frag fondler and fastballing the MAT 50 displayer, Joe Brown knew he might not be in charge of 504 long. Maybe Charles would smuggle a letter to Jane Fonda out of stockade. Then all three networks, the New York *Times*, Washington *Post* and the weekly "news" magazines would come down on his neck like Dennis Hopper falling off a horse, like a blivit bursting on stone.

But as long as he was in charge of 504, Joe Brown knew, he would *command*. And he would command like an eagle colonel, United States Army. Not like a kiss assy March piloting his chair around Saigon, maneuvering expertly between film stars on tour and putting drunk generals to bed; through the cloud turbulence of investigating doves and baring his teeth for the hawks who came out from Congress.

Still feeling a little assy, like Peck, Brown made them wait, let them seethe, knowing they were expecting a big speech. How the new broom was going to sweep out the manure, shape up the outfit, run fifteen or twenty men a day up with the morning colors, and let them fall off the top of the flagpole to land with their butts squarely planted in the stockade. All very, very well. Provided the 504 had an endless pool of manpower from which to draw and the men were all trained, efficient, motivated, experienced; and thought they were John Wayne; and when you got shot it was always in the meat of the leg or through the shoulder.

Colonel Brown did not make a speech.

He said: "There will be another officers' call in one hour. At that time, I expect every man in this room to look like an officer of the United States Army."

He stepped from the platform and walked down the aisle through the rows of benches in the silence and at the door he said, loudly enough, "King, report to me!"

Captain King had already divined something of his new commander. He reported to Brown three minutes later and, somehow, during the interval between Brown's

27

arrival at the 504th and the present moment, King had shaved, put some kind of drops in his eyes to clear the whites and had on a clean, if not pressed-and-starched, uniform.

Brown told King: "When you are off duty, you can drink as much as you like. OK?"

King smiled coyly, and said, "Yes, sir."

Brown said, "I don't expect you will be off duty more than three consecutive hours for the next six weeks. If you report to me for duty smelling of liquor, I will not be convinced that you are fit for duty. Understand?"

King's face looked crumpled, as though all his teeth had been knocked out, but he managed to say in a steady voice, "Yes, sir; I understand."

Brown let up. "Can you do it?"

"I think so."

"No, I didn't ask you that. Can you *do* it? If you can't, I'll send you on out now, and it won't hurt your career, your reputation. It'll be just one of those things that usually happen when a new commander takes over. He brings in his own people."

King came to attention, and he stared straight into Brown's eyes, and he said, "No, Colonel Brown. I can't do it. I'm a drunk. I'm an after-five alcoholic."

Brown nodded, and said, "Thanks. I didn't bring anyone with me, no one. Can you recommend a replacement within the command?"

"I'd rather not."

"Answer me, King. Is there a suitable man in this command? You know what an adjutant's job is. Is there a man who can handle it?"

"Yes, sir," King looked away, and mumbled, "But he's not readily available."

"Stop mealy-mouthing."

"You've got him locked up in stockade, sir. Lieutenant Walker. He's on the newest list for captain. I just . . . hadn't gotten around to . . ."

Brown jerked his left hand at the telephone on his

28

desk. "Get the MP chief on the phone. Tell him to have Walker delivered here at once."

After King put the phone down, Brown said, "What about the maintenance officer?"

"Are you sure you want to trust the judgment of a drunk, Colonel? And I'm not even a pilot."

"You are also a man with a poor memory. Just five minutes ago, I told you to knock off the mealy-mouth."

"I would say he—the maintenance officer—is either incompetent or accepts bribes. Too many of our ships are too often grounded. It's no secret our pilots don't want to fly missions, but we've only had one case of outright refusal; the rest of the time, the pilots manage somehow to refuse their aircraft, and the maintenance officer never argues with them."

"All right, how is the flight surgeon? Big and easy, too?"

King actually hung his head.

"King?"

"He's my drinking buddy."

"So it doesn't matter. A little cold in the head, minor sinus trouble, pain in the ass . . . grounded. . . ."

"Colonel Brown, you've got to understand—"

"Certainly."

"Please, sir."

"All right."

"Doctor Wright . . . well, sir, he has the same feeling about the war, this war, that most of us have."

"I don't think so."

"I beg your pardon?"

"Bertram Wright is not a stranger to me. In the first place he's a recall. He was educated at army expense and effort during the Korean War. Since then he has probably made, gross, more than a million dollars. But he's got a big case of the ass at the army for asking him to pay off the debt, and he jams it up the army, that nameless, faceless, *enemy* that jerked him away from a lucrative private practice. Tell me how wrong I am."

"Not at all, Colonel. Dr. Wright is bitter."

"So every flight medical he gives amounts to that of civilian-airline-transport-rated-pilot, correct?"

"Yes, sir."

"Even goes through the electro-cardiogram bit?"

"Not unless the pilots request it."

"And most of them do?"

"I have not known any to pass up the opportunity."

"Even men like—what was his name?—Bass? Yes, Bass. What is he, twenty-two years old? Needs a heart check like I need a new rectum." With his hands, Brown inscribed a huge circular motion, then he moved his hands so his right forefinger ran in and out of a circle made by the thumb and forefinger on his right hand. Then he made the motion of a man dealing cards.

King understood immediately: great big fucking deal!

Brown had known flight surgeons of Wright's bent before; the Superman complex, maintain the image. With rare exceptions, flight surgeons were not pilots and few had any desire to become flyers, yet some of them simply took it upon themselves to set physical standards for pilots that perhaps two percent of the healthy men in the world could actually meet.

Obviously, then, Wright was making it easy and simple for flight personnel in 504 to ground themselves. "Doc, I got a little sinus here that's really bugging me. . . . Must just be a bad case of the shits, Doc; wore a trail to the latrine all night. . . . Must've sprained my wrist, Doc, playing volleyball last night. . . . Just can't seem to keep my weight down, Doc; I know it knocks my blood pressure right out the top, but I'm just hungry all the time, nerves I guess. . . ."

True, flying a helicopter was not the same as flying a fixed-wing aircraft. Most military pilots, when they chose to speak the truth and were not concerned with maintaining the image, would admit that the airplanes they flew did not require Captain Marvel or Doc Savage at the controls. Rather, they required men possessing ordinary coordination (chew gum and walk at the same time), at least one good eye that would correct to 20/30 and the ability to read the English language so they could go through the check lists.

Most of these pilots would also readily admit that their wives or mothers and fathers could learn to fly the same airplanes. Certainly, beyond the basics, it became a matter of skill, exceptional coordination, perfect eyesight combined with equally perfect depth perception. But that is the description of the *great* pilot, just as it is the description of a great billiards player, football quarterback, rodeo bronc rider.

It did require somewhat better coordination, either natural or developed, to fly a helicopter, than it required to fly fixed-wing aircraft; and that was the only difference. Mother could learn to fly a *CH 34 Choctaw*, too; but it would take longer than soloing a *Cessna 150*.

So Flight Surgeon Wright had to go, he and his airline-transport-rating medical examinations that exceeded the manual he was supposed to be working from. Hell, over in another squadron there was an old warrant-officer pilot with arrested glaucoma who was still on flight status and going on missions every day. Wright had to go or Brown would never get 504 airborne.

He took care of it, immediately. While King went to Wright's office and told him to pack his gear, Brown got on the horn and after all the buzzing and popping and delays, he reached March in HQ, Saigon. "Send me a flight surgeon that believes in men flying."

"I've got one on the way, Joe. We know Wright's reputation up here and knew you'd want to get rid of him."

Brown was surprised, and for a moment, couldn't speak.

March said, "Joe, we know we handed you a shitty and perhaps impossible job; but we *are* going to make every effort to help you get the job done."

"You're proving it, and thanks."

"What else?"

31

"One thing I'm asking as a personal favor. Don't ruin the careers of any men I run off this base. Make them transfers. I'll play the role of the villain. New broom, came in and cleaned out all the old boys."

"Will do. Anything else?"

"Not right now, but find me a good chief of maintenance, just in case I need one in a hurry."

"Got it. What else?"

"That's endgate. You got anything for me?"

"Doctor Elmore will be there within the hour."

Brown thanked March and rang off as King rapped on the door and then entered, followed by Dr. Wright. "I demand to know the reason for being relieved of duty!"

With deceptive mildness, Brown said, "You are not being relieved; you are being transferred."

"Don't give me that—"

"I'll give you something, all right, *Doctor*. One opportunity to take off that stupid hat with the cowpuncher-roll, then stand at attention, report properly, salute and, then, get your ass out of here. Because you are leaving within the hour, either transferred or in handcuffs and leg-irons, as a prisoner under arrest, for gross and flagrant conduct unbecoming an officer and direct disobedience to multiple orders." Brown walked across the office and stopped before the doctor, who had jerked off his hat, stood at rigid attention and held his hand to his eyebrow, saying with fluttering lips, "Major Bertram Wright reporting as ordered to the commanding officer, sir."

"Not quite correct. You were not ordered here. You were ordered to pack your gear for transportation to Saigon."

"Yes, sir."

"Now you decide, Major. You can be lolling back in the officers' club with a drink in your hand and hatred in your heart; or you can be in a cell with the stink of urine in your nostrils and fear eating up your guts."

Brown turned his back on Wright, saying, "Dismissed."

King sounded like a man trying to talk fast enough

to get something said before he had to run and vomit. "Sir, Lieutenant Walker is waiting."

"Bring him— No, send him in. Without any MP escort."

Brown went to his desk and stood with his right hip resting against it. Walker came into the office stiffly, eyes straight ahead, stopped, saluted, reported. Brown said, "How do you feel?"

"I'm all right."

"You won't be all right for a week. Your urine's black and you feel like someone's twisting a knife inside your liver."

Walker didn't say anything. He stared straight ahead. Brown pawed through the papers on King's messy desk and found the list. "Did you know you are a captain now?"

"I thought I was a prisoner."

Brown said, "Look at me," and he felt the impact of the hatred of the piercing blue eyes when Walker turned his face and looked at Brown. "Whether you are a prisoner or promoted to captain is entirely up to you."

"I don't get it."

"King's out. He's a drunk, a procrastinator, but he is a man and proved it, by admitting what I've just told you. I need a replacement for him. He recommended you."

"Shit!"

"How'd you like the next one right up under the heart, kid? Or across the throat, so you talk whispers the rest of your life?"

"You wouldn't dare. The only reason you might, just *might*, get by with knocking me out at the airport is because I made the mistake of trying to shove you away from standing on my toes."

"No witnesses."

"Captain King and two MPs are just outside the door."

"And they will believe precisely what I tell them to believe."

"That I attacked you and you—defended yourself. . . ."

33

"Do you want to work for me or not?"

Walker did not answer.

"Have you got a watch?"

"Huh—"

"The word is sir."

"No, sir. They took everything, even my bootlaces, at the stockade."

Brown took off his watch and held it up before Walker's eyes. "Within the next fifty minutes a helicopter will land here with a new flight surgeon to replace Major Wright, who has been transferred. You take this watch and go out there in the hallway and sit down on that bench. You have exactly thirty minutes from right now to decide if you want to become a captain and adjutant of 504, or if you want about ten years on the rockpile at Leavenworth." Brown stepped past Walker and opened the door.

The MPs came to attention. Brown told them, "You guys grab a cup of coffee or something. Mr. Walker's going to be here with me for a while."

Walker sat down on the bench and took the watch, in a daze. Brown left him there and asked King, "Are the men in the briefing room for that second officers' call?"

"Yes, Colonel; they've been waiting for some time."

There was a noticeable improvement, but as there always are among any group of men, there were the few who did not have the nerve to defy outright, but left little bits and pieces of "messages" indicating defiance. Just to let *The Man* know they were independent souls possessing "human dignity." And there were two who simply showed complete and utter defiance and made sure Brown saw them, by sitting on the first row of benches directly in front of the briefing platform.

For the time being, Brown ignored them. To the assembled officers, he said, "You are at least beginning to look like human beings. But in this room we hold briefings only for flight personnel of the 504th. There will be another briefing at midnight, at which time I will see if

34

any soldiers report. If so, at that time we will commence the business of functioning as a military unit."

He paused for a moment, and then said, "There will not be one single further warning. Get rid of the beads, sandals and hair, the symbols, decals and patches, the headbands and all the other crap."

Brown then pointed down at the two men directly in front of him. "You two overdid it. You don't get the second chance. You are under arrest." Brown raised his voice. "Excepting these two men, the remainder of you are dismissed."

As the others began to file out, muttering and mumbling, Brown stepped down off the platform and stopped before the pair. "Names?"

"Hopler," said the one on the left; he smelled like a hog.

"Bynum," answered the other, who smelled like a dead hog.

Brown had expected them to carry it all the way through, so he was not angered, nor surprised, when neither man rose to salute and report properly.

"Hopler, what's your job?"

"Helicopter pilot."

"Rank?"

"Warrant officer."

"Age?"

"Twenty-one."

"And this pile of stinking shit is one of your crewmen, right?"

Brown saw the flashing flush of anger in their attitudes; he could not see any reddening of skin; they were both too dirty.

"How about it, Bynum? You're a sergeant, a gunner."

Sullenly, Bynum nodded.

"OK, let's go." Brown gestured, pointing toward the far door of the briefing room. The men looked at one another, and Brown saw that Bynum was waiting for some kind of signal from Hopler. Brown said, "Don't try it. I can take you both, here, now, anytime, everyplace. I'll kill you before I'll let you hurt me."

That did it for Hopler. He put his hands on his thighs so they would be in plain sight and clearly no threat, and he got to his feet. Bynum sighed; it was the sound of a man who has just missed a near-collision in an automobile. Glad to be alive. Brown followed them out and told them to go on to King's office. As they went inside ahead of Brown, Brown shot a look at Walker. Man on death row. Head shaved, electrodes attached, chair waiting . . . at least twenty of his desperate minutes had passed, sitting there alone in the gloomy hallway. Brown knew with a certainty what Walker must have been thinking: do the obvious, agree, take the job, then screw up the whole works, so 504 and its new colonel look even worse than before. Brown knew that was the chance he was taking and he could not, honestly, hope to predict the outcome. He did not know Walker well enough—the man's drives, motives, ambitions, objectives in life. But Brown did know Walker was tough and hard. He was man enough to show his defiance like a man, not like the hogs in King's office. He had pride; he looked Brown and the world straight in the eye. There had to be something to him. Brown only hoped Walker was not one of those crazily-stubborn ones, the kind so filled with pride that he just very god damn well might choose to do hard-time in an army penitentiary to show Brown he couldn't be forced, or blackmailed. Brown had already admitted to himself that what he'd proposed to Walker was simple extortion . . . of the kind practiced daily in the army and every other military service and in every corporate relationship. At least it wasn't quite like the opposition: try to be a rebel and see what and where it gets you over there. Siberia, if you're lucky. And if you're not, kneeling with your hands wired behind your back while a hero of the revolution shoots holes through the back of your head. Brown went to Walker and took back his watch. He looked down at the young man sitting on the bench.

36

Brown said, "When you hear the ship coming in to land, come into my office and tell me what you have decided to do."

Walker nodded and Brown went into King's office and shut the door, wondering what he was going to do with this filthy pair, Hopler and Bynum. King was standing there, too, waiting, with his face wrinkled with revulsion at the odors off the two men.

Brown said, "Leave the door open and turn on that fan and open the window. Get a bottle of shaving lotion or something to spray around so we can stand the stink." He shot a look at the pair; they were grinning; they thought they were winning. As King moved about the room doing what Brown had ordered, Brown said, "As your last official act, draw up my first new order. All flight crews are hereby disbanded. There is too much buddy-buddy stuff in this outfit, and it's one thing that's caused a lot of the trouble."

Brown shot another look at the pair of hogs, and they no longer had that winners' smirk; they looked stricken.

King sat down at his desk and began to draw the order in longhand.

"What the hell are you doing? Don't you have a clerk-typist?"

"He doesn't like to take dictation."

"Now that's what I call—" Brown could not finish. He shouted. "Get him! Here! Now!"

King left, and a few moments later returned. Swishing along behind King came a young man so obviously and aggressively homosexual that he minced as he walked. He looked like a hard blonde playing a cheap whore in an old B movie; all he lacked was the swinging purse.

Brown actually felt like pulling the pistol from his waistband above his left hip and shooting the queer through the face, six times. Brown managed to say, "I won't ask what your problem is." The clerk arched his eyebrows, and in a deadly level voice, Brown said, "Get your gear and take down Captain King's order as he

37

dictates it to you. I will expect it to be ready for my signature in five minutes."

Brown swung around to the sniggering Hopler and Bynum, but before he could speak, he heard the thudding blades of a descending helicopter. He turned toward the door and a moment later Walker came into the room.

5

Brown leaned against his desk with his arms folded. Walker looked around the room with obvious discomfort, and Brown said, "The rest of you wait in the hall. King, keep your eye on this pair. You, too, sweetheart, get your flaky bum out. Find another office and finish typing King's order."

Hopler and Bynum went out, followed by the swishy clerk and Captain King. Brown did not move. The noise of the helicopter increased for a moment, then diminished as it settled to the ground, and the only sound was of the turbines winding down.

Brown did not say anything. He matched Walker's blue stare. Then Walker drew himself up, breathed deeply, and said, "I'll take the job."

"That's all I wanted to hear, Captain. You can go get your gear packed and ride out with King and Major Wright."

The astonishment made Walker's face fall apart. "But, sir, I thought—"

"Not a chance. I don't work with men I have to hold a knife over and I'm afraid to turn my back to."

"But I didn't—"

"Are you sure?"

"Sir, you're— You're going too fast for me." Walker put his hands up to his face and scrubbed out his eyes with the heels of his hands. "I guess I'm just tired."

"Sit down."

Walker took the chair near the corner of the desk and Brown looked down at him, the tired slump of thin worn shoulders, the grime on the pilot's hands, the faint blond stubbly beard. "How many times you been out, Walker?"

"I think I've lost track. Seventy, seventy-six missions. I don't—"

"No, I mean how many tours does this make for you?"

"It's my third."

"This is my fifth, and I crawled out of a honeymoon bed to get here."

"Jesus, sir, I—"

"OK, now we've sung our sad songs to one another, let's get it straight. I appreciate your offering to stay on. I don't think it was because you were really afraid of prison. You could have beaten it. If not at your trial, then certainly on appeal. Agreed?"

"Yes, sir, I thought about that." He smiled, just a slight bending of the lips, like a man so tired he's silently asking permission not to be made to talk. But Walker did speak. "I don't think you'd ever have brought it up, charges and specs. I finally figured out what you were doing. You had to start someplace, and at the beginning is always the best place."

Brown nodded, and asked, "Are you putting the con on me?"

"Sir—?"

"Giving me all the breaks of it, rationalizing it out for me, then after you've slipped around quietly and gotten depositions and signed eye-witness statements from your crew, you drop the sky on my skull."

The question, which Brown deliberately made sound like an accusation, angered Walker so greatly the pilot shot up from the chair, fists doubled, and only with the greatest effort of will did not quite throw a punch.

Brown grinned at him, an invitation. Walker swallowed and sighed, and then he slacked back into the chair, like a used-up rag. After a moment, Brown found some cigarettes on King's desk and offered them. Walker took one and Brown lighted it, then one for himself even as he told himself, Go ahead, dumbutt, turn up the flame under that ulcer!

Brown said, "Time's eating us up. Give me one motive for staying with me, one single reason I can accept, and

40

the job is yours. Otherwise, you're going out with the rest of the trash under the broom."

"Do you think I *like* looking this way?" Walker gestured down at his length. "Cruddy? Do you think I want to live and eat and sleep with a bunch of animal-like creeps? That I *like* being in an outfit that's infected with some kind of disease I can't even define? That I *like* finding out all the great and noble stuff they passed out like ice cream back at Huntsville and Hood and Saigon HQ—"

"Take it easy."

"All right . . . I know there is something *wrong* here. This unit has taken a lot of casualties, had slack leadership, let it slip and slide until it's not a military unit any longer; it's a bunch of bums. I came into the army to fly airplanes. That's all. I came in to get a free aviation education, and when my time's up I'm leaving and not looking back and putting in my application for every airline in the world. I already got all my tickets, ATR, instrument, the whole smash, last time I was stateside. When I'm out and gone I'm after that two-thousand-dollar-a-month stuff. Where you sit up there in the cockpit and sing cowboy songs or tell war stories while a flight director flies the big son of a bitch, and I pick up the microphone and tell the passengers there's really no such thing as an airpocket, it's clear air turbulence."

Walker got to his feet. "But I'm not there yet. I'm *here*, and as long as I am *here*, I want to do it with some god damn class, not like a bunch of common sons of bitches who spit on the floor and never answer their mail!"

"Captain, you're hired." Brown stuck out his hand and they shook.

Brown said, "Give me a quick list of priorities. What's the worst thing wrong with this outfit."

"The rotten friggin chow, so far as I'm concerned."

"That figures. That's *always* part of it, a big part of it, with any unit going downhill."

"That hardnosed flight surgeon—"

41

"He's gone."

"The NCOIC, the chief enlisted man on the base does nothing but keep his eye on the EM club. I'm convinced he's stealing it blind. The men believe the same. He's selling great chow in the club, and I think he's buying it from the cook. Then there are the girls. . . ."

"OK, we've got a start. Tell me, truthfully, how bad is the drug problem in 504."

"It is very, very bad. It all fits in, doesn't it, sir? With the whole atmosphere, the slackness, the dirty, nastiness of it all?"

"Exactly." Brown paused a moment, then asked, "Who was the pilot I've heard about who refused to fly, the only outright refusal?"

"Colonel, I give you one guess."

"Hopler."

"Right on."

"Do you know why? Is he a coward, or a commie, or what?"

"He's strung out so bad on drugs he can't fly. He actually did everyone a favor when he refused. He'd have gone in, lost the ship and crew."

Brown nodded and looked at his watch. His eyes stung, and he felt a pulling strain across his thick shoulders. There had been a time in his life when Joe Brown said, truthfully, he'd never been tired, drunk, sick, hungover or homesick. But now at the age of forty-two, and with that lousy ulcer poisoning his system and its pain tiring him, he would not have wanted to try to put that claim to a real test. But like they said back in the ranching country where he was raised, "If you're going to be a cowpuncher, you've got to learn to get your sleep in the wintertime."

He looked down at Walker and saw a fatigue matching his own, but Walker was a young man, should have another three days in him; but to set a tone, to establish a relationship, to let Walker know that his commander did care, Brown asked, "Can you make it the rest of the night?"

Walker grinned. "If I can't make it, Colonel, then I'll hang my wings on it and cry."

"Let's go."

When Brown came out into the hallway, King handed over the first of Brown's new orders. Brown signed left handed and gave the papers to the clerk. "Run off copies and post them. You have an hour."

"Tonight?"

"Not tonight. Within an hour." Brown went on down the hallway, and met the new flight surgeon coming in, Major Elmore. They shook hands and Brown took the doctor aside. "The first thing I want, set it up tonight, use the MPs, is urine samples from every man in the unit."

"Bad drug problem?"

"Appears so, including at least one of the officers."

"Key-rist."

"I'd test your own staff first, if I were you. They have access more readily than most of the others."

"Will do, which reminds me; I kidnapped my two best men and brought them along."

Brown motioned Walker over. "Get some instant transfer orders in motion for the names Doc Elmore gives you. Doc, this is Captain Walker, the new 504 adjutant."

Brown passed on out and went to the messhall, Walker catching up to him, trying to scribble names in a notebook by the light of the moon. They caught all the messhall crew asleep except two drunken cooks trying to arm-wrestle on a filthy butcherblock in the kitchen. Brown went to a wall fire hydrant, wrapped his hand in his hat, broke the glass, spun the valve open and started hosing down everything in sight, particularly the two drunks. He moved through the deepening water across the nasty, slick floor and kicked open doors as he came to them, knocking men from their beds with the force of the jetting water. When he found the Mess Sergeant, an all-too-typical type, with the boozer's face and huge, pendulous gut, Brown kept knocking the fat man down every time he tried to get to his feet. In the blast of water, in his pain, fright and anger, Sergeant Morris couldn't tell,

43

probably could not even imagine who, in God's name, would have the nerve to do such a thing so his curses rose to a rich, high volume and exhibited great originality.

Brown snapped off the nozzle valve and let Sergeant Jack Morris wipe the water from his eyes and take a look. Mess Sergeant Morris went the dead-white color of a man who has just seen Jesus come down off the cross, point his finger directly into Jack Morris' face, and say, "Stick me with a spear, will you?"

Morris tried to salute. Brown kept from laughing but Walker had to stuff his hand in his mouth and turn away. Morris stood naked but for thin white GI shorts pasted wetly to his body, his monstrous sagging gut hanging over the top band of the shorts. What made him look most ridiculous of all was the fact that Morris had girlish legs, almost shapely calves and trim ankles, that ended in big wide flat hairy feet.

Colonel Brown said, "You have an hour." Then turned away. Morris came running after Brown. "Sir, sir, an hour for *what*?"

Walker stopped and smiled and placed a gentle hand on Morris' fat wet shoulder. "To get the place ready for inspection, to prepare breakfast, to have your account books ready for audit and whatever else you might think the Colonel would like to take a look at when he returns."

They found the NCOIC, Senior Sergeant Major Kelley, in bed with two Viet girls. Kelley lay on his back. One of the girls sat astraddle his face, the other had his penis in her mouth. The scene seemed to freeze, after a moment, because when Brown first opened the door and stepped inside, followed by Walker, and turned on the light, the participants in the little game were too busy to notice. The Viet girl atop Kelley's face became aware first. She screamed as she leaped off the bed and tried to curl herself into a tiny ball behind a highbacked chair. Kelley half-raised up, muttering, "What'n hell—" and, then, he looked worse than Mess Sergeant Morris did when he thought Jesus spoke to him. The other girl was last to notice, and reluctant to stop. Brown had a thought that,

44

perhaps, she put on exhibitions and having the lights on and viewers standing and watching was nothing new to her. But, then of course, she soon had nothing to work with, Kelley having come to that state which is sometimes, with intended humor, called an "Irish peter:" gone to Dublin.

The second girl had a little more class, or poise, than the first. She did not curl up and hide. She stood up, slipped into a silk gown and sat down in the chair behind which the other girl hid. Brown did not say anything, nor did Walker; they only looked at Kelley, and then at one another. There was no use telling Kelley he was under arrest, charged with sodomy. You can't put a dead man on trial. For, while the second girl rose and robed, Kelley bucked up once, hard and high, arching. Then his left arm flung out and jerked upwards as his right arm came across his chest. Hugging himself he said, "Oh, God! No!" as the heart attack took him and delivered him to whatever or wherever that place is over there on The Other Side.

Without instructions from Brown, Walker went across to the desk in one corner of Kelley's room and used the telephone. The MPs arrived first to take the girls into custody, to get statements from them; the medics came a few moments later and took charge of the remains. Brown told the MP sergeant to get on his radio in the jeep and have a CID crew sent over to start the criminal investigation of Kelley's alleged activities. Then Brown went into the EM lounge and behind the bar and got down a bottle of Old Parr and found clean glasses, looked at Walker with a question expressed on his face. Walker nodded and Brown poured out two big ones, added a dash of water. They lit smokes and leaned against the bar, facing one another, and sipped and smoked without talking until the drinks were finished. It was ten minutes past midnight.

In the briefing room, the flyers waited. The *word* was out; it had gotten around; the 504th had been transported far beyond the northern sea, just as in the old song. Except it was not "Ruben, Ruben" up there on the plat-

45

form, this was not the bottom of the sea, the men of the 504th had not been waiting and there was no girl singing the song.

The news was out. All over town.

The 504th might, possibly, never again fly a single mission, perhaps not even a training flight; but it was already, in just nine hours, beginning to resemble, to a considerable degree, an aviation unit of the United States Army.

If there was any song, that was it: "You Win Again."

Because the news was damned sure out, all over town. There was this green-eyed, lefthanded, Indian-looking eagle colonel who had come down on this cruddy 504 outfit like a ton of chickenshit off a twenty-story building. And it was getting all over everyone in sight, and all it looked like getting was worse. Hell, they might even have to start flying missions again!

Brown stood on the platform and looked them over, with Walker at his side. And he cut his eyes so he could look at Walker, and he saw a young man not standing up there with a "Gee, fellers, what can I do?" attitude, but a hard-faced copy of Brown. Walker had hired out, and he was doing the job. To the men, Brown said, "The resemblance is vague, but clearly discernible. I think you people have returned, from whatever filth-rotten place you've been, and come back into the army."

Joe Brown looked at his watch. It was 0025 hours—twenty-five minutes past midnight. "Breakfast at zero five hundred hours. Sleep fast, men; it'll be here soon."

As he passed out through the corridor down between the rows of benches, Brown heard some unknown voice say, "God damn, it don't take long to spend a night with that son of a bitch, does it?"

Brown told Walker to peel off and take care of the paperwork that had to be done to cover the many things they had done in the past few hours, and then Brown went back to the messhall. Fat Morris stood around screaming his head off, issuing so many and so frequently-contradictory orders that his men moved sluggishly about

46

in a daze. A man mopping the floor might suddenly have to drop his mop and grab a cloth and start wiping a table. When Brown entered the room far enough so that Morris saw him, the fat sergeant began visibly trembling. Brown walked back to the kitchen. It was cleaner but still caked with old grease and congealed spillings. A huge vessel sat over a pair of burners and Brown went to it. Inside bubbled a sticky, globby mass. Brown turned to Morris. "What is this tub of shit?"

"Oatmeal, sir!" Morris said, saluting. He had dressed in Class-A summer-weights, including a necktie. Brown raised up his long left leg and kicked the vat over. The oatmeal inside did not spill out and run across the floor. It hit with a wet *thut*, and then, slowly, began spreading in all directions like some kind of glob in a science-fiction movie, some alien "thing" threatening to consume earth and all its beings.

Morris stood like a man with all his thongs cut, slumped and defeated and utterly boneless. Brown said, "Come with me," and walked back to Morris' private room. Brown shut the door and told Morris to sit down. Morris sat on the very edge of his bunk, as though ready to make a serious attempt to turn a back flip through his own rectum if the colonel so ordered. Brown caught him from the blind side. "Got anything to drink?"

Morris was caught so unawares that he stuttered, and he never did answer. He finally just bent over and pulled a footlocker from under his bunk and opened it with a key and did not even try to block Brown's view of the fifty bottles of whisky inside the lockerbox. "Any special—"

"Old Parr Scotch," Brown said. Morris got out one of the squatty, square bottles, found glasses, poured.

"How long you been in, Morris?"

"Nearly thirty years, sir."

"Ever been shot at?"

"I was infantryman in the Big War, made Anzio, landed at Normandy."

"How'd you get to be such a pig?"

"Just riding along, I guess. I never was one of the gung-ho guys. I just done my job. Decided to get back in after I couldn't find a job in '46, and went to cook'n' baker school."

"No combat in Korea?"

"No, sir. I was rated cook by then. Back'n' rear with the gear."

"But what made you a thief?"

"I'm no thief, sir, begging your pardon, but by God now, sir—"

"Where did you get the booze?"

"I traded— I mean, well, sir—"

"You had a deal with Kelley."

Morris found it necessary to inspect the toes of his scuffed shoes.

"You traded off government-issued rations, the good stuff: meat, eggs, all that, to Kelley. In return, he gave you all the booze you wanted. You couldn't possibly drink all that, not even a hollow-leg like you, so you've had a sideline. Every so often, when you know it's safe, you hitch a ride up to the lines, and carry along a case or two and peddle it to the infantrymen. Fifty, seventy-five dollars a bottle. You make the rounds of the rear-echelon-aid stations and hospitals. Tell me, Morris, were you *really* offended when I called you a thief?"

"No, sir." Morris had eyes the blue color of a sky with a high thin overcast, washed out, with the whites heavily and permanently bloodshot. "Sir, please, I couldn't stand going to stockade, please, sir. What can I do?"

"Make it right."

"But . . . but, sir, *how*?"

"All right, listen to me. And you whisky-soaked son of a bitch, if you think you can't remember it, *take notes!*"

"I'll remember, sir, I promise."

"The first thing you do is go over there and clean out that EM club. Everything but the booze over there came from here in the first place. Don't worry about audits, responsibility, any of that crap. In case you hadn't heard your old henchman is dead."

48

"Kelley's dead?"

"Heart attack." Brown didn't smile but he could not help thinking, And what a way to go! "The CID has the place sealed, has his books, records, everything. But I'll fix it so when you go over with your men to get all the chow, it will be a matter of Kelley storing the stuff for you. You recently had some freezer problems."

"Yeah, yeah—I mean, yes, sir! That orter work OK. Yes, sir."

"Now fatman, are you ready for the crunch?"

Morris just stared at Brown, dumbly.

"This outfit keeps *on* getting fed like at the Carriage Room at Hilton Inn in Tucson, and it's all on you."

Morris had that Jesus-coming-down look again. He finally managed to say, "Sir, I don't have any of that money left, that I made selling the whisky, like you said I did."

"Where is it?"

"I lost it. I got this gambling thing. . . ."

But Brown saw the same sliding-off-of-eyes look in Morris that he'd seen in Saigon, talking to March. Where did all this shit come from anyway, Brown wondered, the blue-eyed propaganda? Pilots, gunfighters, movie stars, all that crap. Brown picked it up very high and held it over Jack Morris' head, and let it fall. "You're lying. I *know* you're lying. You've got it cached, you've bought into a business, either here in Vietnam or back Stateside, something. You're lying." Brown paused for just a second, then said, "But just in case you are not, if the money is gone, then Morris, you had better learn how to eat paper, drink green and black ink, and *shit* the money to replace what's been stolen and traded off, or you are going to the stockade."

Brown knew he let a streak of mean come out when he really savaged Morris by adding, "You couldn't make it in stockade, Morris. You'd either kill yourself, or in six months they'd make a raving fag out of you."

Head down, body totally slack, fat wobbling as he moved, Morris nodded his head. "It will take a few days,

49

Colonel, but I'll have the money back, and I'll use it as you said."

"One more thing."

"Yes, sir?"

"You have one week to prove to me that you *are* a mess sergeant. That you can run this mess, feed my men, keep the place spotless; a week. If you can't, then you're up for courtmartial, busted to grunt for inefficiency, sent to a line company. That's a hard way to go for a man almost fifty years old and a hundred-fifty pounds over his weight."

At zero five fifteen hours, fifteen minutes past five o'clock that morning, Brown and Walker went into the messhall. The floors were reasonably clean, the tables spotless. On the serving line stood trays of thick ham, ham and cheese, fried egg, and other varieties of sandwiches. The sound of the eating men had a happy, contented, almost wondrous tone to it. Brown passed through the line, got a ham and cheese sandwich and a cup of black coffee, went over and found a seat with some unknown enlisted men at one of the tables. The coffee was excellent, the sandwich passable; but Brown knew that Morris had not had much time to prepare, so forgave him.

Walker came in, got a cup of coffee and sat down beside Brown and reported he'd just come from the officers' mess, and there was the same noticeable improvement. Brown finished his food, drank his coffee, told Walker, "Let's hit the flight line."

6

Captain Ray Marston was another blue-eyed man. Colonel Joe Brown knew he'd come to hate men with blue eyes, with complete unjustifiability and unreasoning emotion. It was like hating blacks, or Viets, or girls with small bosoms, simply because they existed, and not because of the individuals.

But the man stood before him exhibiting every symptom of "get me if you can" defiance. Joe Brown did not say anything. He looked at the man and he could not understand why he felt such unreasoning dislike for a man he had never seen before. He knew he had been hard, almost savage, to some of the others he'd had to shape up in the past fifteen hours, but there was nothing personal in any of it. So this with Marston bothered Joe Brown, and then he realized what it was, and it actually had nothing to do with Marston, himself, at all. . . .

He and Jody had been in the Carriage Room of the Hilton Inn at Tucson. It was already decided. They would get married Monday. They could hardly touch their food for looking into one another's eyes and the waiter kept hovering around the table in a frenzy of, "Isn't the food properly prepared?"

Joe Brown, dressed in civilian clothes, assured the waiter that everything was just fine, which allowed the waiter to hustle off to another table nearby, over near the wall where the booths were, and care for the needs of a loud and demanding group of motion-picture people. Some outfit called Coaltown, or something like that, was in town and making the Hilton its headquarters. All the tourist types kept cricking their necks to see The Famous

51

Movie Star, and his equally Famous Movie Star Wife, when they came in to dinner, without realizing that FMS and FMSW always ate in their suite because they did not have any desire (and it bugged them like hell) to mix with the people who had made them both millionaires before either of them passed the age of thirty.

Knowledgeable people, of course, recognized the lower echelons, those with feature billings, the ones whose names appear down the list of names so far that if you own an old-fashioned or small-screen television set, you can't even see their names. Then—since this was a pseudo-western—the wranglers, animal trainers and caretakers, and the stuntmen swaggered about in their uniform: thin nylon windbreakers, long-sleeved shirts, usually striped, wide belts with rodeo trophy buckles, whether earned personally or not, jeans and sweat-socks with racers—a kind of soft-soled track shoe, with stripes down the instep sides. In a lot of cases, so no one would make any mistake about whom they saw, the behind-the-scenes people wore cheap white jackets or vests with the name of The Famous Movie Star and/or his wife, and the name of the movie in which FMS was soon to appear. Of course, the guy wearing the jacket or the vest might be one of the hired help who kept the horseshit swept off the sand where the next scene was to be filmed, but the jacket did identify him as "one of those in the Industry." Which was, of course, what they always called it: the Industry. Never the picture business, or movie business, or motion-picture business, unless they were putting on one of the stupes—the paying customers who attended movies and kept them working—then they were in "moom-pitchers." Laugh up the cuff.

The whisky and water had gone to work on Joe Brown and he needed to make a trip, so he excused himself from Jody at the table, touched her shoulder going past, and went over toward the bar and passed along it toward the lobby. He noticed but did not pay any attention to the extremely husky, rather short man with thick black hair at the bar, who seemed to make a point of staring straight into Brown's eyes as he passed. The man, Joe noticed, wore the "uniform," jeans, racers, thick white socks, black shirt with white stripes, dark nylon windbreaker; typical Hollywood stud, all white teeth and inch-deep tan. Brown, still feeling the twinges of his last wound, in the hip, and washed out pale from too much inside time at the hospital, must not have looked like the man who should be that marvelous brown-eyed woman's date. The moment Brown went out of sight around the corner into the lobby and toward the men's room, the Hollywood told the bartender, "Put that on the company tab, my room number," picked up his drink and went directly to the table where Jody sat.

Jody sipped her vodka and tonic and looked around the room. She noticed with a sort of weary-readiness-to-endure, what the next show was about to bring: it would be the same little fat girl with her mouth full of capped teeth who did the same routine four times every evening, her big production number being "Fiddler on the Roof."

Jody took another sip, lit a cigarette, and only then became aware of the shadow that fell across her face. She looked up, smiling, not expecting Joe back so soon.

It wasn't Joe.

Instead, it was the Hollywood type she could not help noticing earlier who'd sat at the bar, stripping her naked with his eyes. She didn't like men looking at her like that, except certain men, but over the past twenty-few years, she had become accustomed to it; it was something many men did, and if done properly it was a sort of compliment. She did not like the way this man had stared at her from the bar, and she did not like the way he looked at her now.

"Hiya, babe," the Hollywood said.

Jody shot a look at the door, but Joe was nowhere in sight.

"What's a bunch of woman like you doing with an old jerk like that?"

Jody saw her knuckles grow white, holding her glass,

and she managed to keep her voice low and level. "Get the hell out of here."

"Hey, come on now," the Hollywood showed all his teeth, contrasting the incredible whiteness of the perfect caps against the darkness of his suntan.

"Go hustle someone your own age, buster." Jody jerked her head toward the singer. The Hollywood type just laughed. He said, "You're my kind of woman, babe; mature."

"Going to do me a favor, huh?"

"Something like that, if you say so. I saw the creep you're with when he left. What was it, kidney trouble? Like most old men?" The Hollywood made a production of staring at Jody's full bosoms. She raised her arms and put her hands under her chin so that her forearms blocked his view. "Hey!" the Hollywood said. "Don't hide them!"

He put both doubled fists down on the table and leaned over her, and she could smell the drink on his breath, and the Hollywood said, "How's let's split from the old creep before he gets back, huh? Go over to my room, fool around a little, see a few pictures I've had taken time to time," he flashed the white again, "you know? The Polaroids. Then we ball it up a while, like all the rest of the night. Except I got to get out early." His chest swelled. "I'm in the picture we're making, you know."

The Hollywood grinned again, and maybe he was looking beyond Jody and watching his own beautiful face in the crackly-finish mirror on the wall above the booths, because he missed the expression of utter relief on Jody's face when she saw Joe coming. All she remembered was the Hollywood saying something more, a sentence or, at most, two, then reaching past her arm to touch her full left breast because, at that moment, Joe stopped beside the table.

Joe had seen something wrong as he came back into the room, the pained, almost frightened expression on Jody's face, the way she would not look at the man standing over her at the table and how she shook her head. He made his way almost rudely through the crush of people and got there just as the Hollywood put his hand on Jody. Joe did not say anything. He did not ask what's the problem here, or Jody is this guy bugging you, because he had already recalled that Jody had seemed uncomfortable at the table a few times earlier and twice had shifted her chair. He remembered the uniformed Hollywood giving him the long look as Joe passed the bar going to the toilet, so Joe understood at once. In the parlance of his trade, he evaluated the situation at once. He could not trust his left hand and he knew just from looking that the Hollywood was in marvelous physical condition, so Joe took it from him without giving the Hollywood any chance for an advantage.

Joe skipped forward and kicked the man as hard as he could on the left kneecap; under the toe of his hard-soled shoe, Joe felt the inside of the man's knee turn to a bagful of assorted bone chips. When the Hollywood bent to grab his knee, screaming, Joe caught the man's mop of black hair in his right hand, twisted it for a solid grip and jerked the teeth-filled face downwards as he brought his right knee up, driving it in as hard as he could. He had to support the Hollywood's weight because the man could not stand on that leg with the destroyed knee; and Joe smashed his own knee into the other's face again. Then he felt someone wrap his arms around him from the back, pull him away, and say, "Jesus, man, that's plenty. There's no use killing him."

Joe spun around inside the clasping arms ready to drive the knee upwards into a crotch, but the other Hollywood was too quick and wise. At the same time that he moved back fast from Joe, he shoved Joe's shoulders and said, "I don't want to fight. It's all over. Christ, look at him."

The Hollywood lay on the floor, crying. It sounded wet and thick, coming through all the bubbling blood, crushed nose and broken teeth; and Hollywood could not decide which place deserved most attention, his knee or his face. Because Joe Brown did not understand the Hollywood mentality, that you treat people like shit who can no longer be of use to you, he expected to have to fight them all, then. All the guy's pals, buddies, colleagues and whoever else wanted to pile on the heap. But he did not have to fight them. That's how the man's buddies carried him out, like a bag of shit, one on each arm, one with each foot, ignoring his screams of pain. He was no longer of any use to them, because in his condition he could no longer work on the picture in progress.

And now, here at the maintenance shops and hangars of 504, Joe Brown found his maintenance officer so like the Hollywood that night in Tucson that he had to turn away from him and trim up the balance before he could bring himself to speak to the man. Joe thought it would probably be a good thing to fire the man at once, bring in a replacement. He had enough to worry about without personal hatred for a man he did not know, except by poor recommendation and reputation. But Joe Brown did not command by thinking about how a man parted his hair or wore sunglasses indoors so everyone would know he was an airman, or because his teeth were spaced too far apart, so he made himself put out his hand and say, "Colonel Joe Brown. You're Marston, the maintenance officer."

"Yes, sir."

"Let's talk. Where's your office?"

They went inside the hangar, and Brown liked what he saw. The benches and tools were clean, so was the floor; but most of the men were idle, so then Brown did not like what he saw.

Once inside, Marston offered and then poured coffee; they lit cigarettes. Brown sipped, puffed, then tore into Marston. "Why can't you keep the aircraft flying?"

A deep red flush of anger flooded up Marston's neck and his lips turned white with suppressed words. After a moment, he said, "I can make fly anything designed to go into the air."

"You haven't."

"It's the pilots, not me."

"Who's your test pilot?"

"I have none, and haven't had for seven weeks."

"Why do you allow the pilots to refuse aircraft when you *know* they are perfectly safe and ready?"

"You can answer that better than I can, Colonel. It's in the book, *aircraft commander*. It doesn't make a damn if he's a boot warrant or wet-eared second lieutenant, if he's the pilot, then he is *in command* of his aircraft. If he says the son of a bitch can't go, he does not have to take it."

"He's got to have a reason."

"God damn it, there's always a reason. There's no such thing as a *perfect* aircraft, everytime. A little too much drop on one mag, a little engine roughness because it sat at idle too long with rich mixture and the plugs loaded up, or he *hears* something that doesn't sound *quite right*." Marston wiped his mouth. "Shit! Some punks don't know—"

"Why is there no test pilot?"

"We don't have one qualified . . . by the book, I mean."

"That's a regulation that's ignored all over the god damn world, Marston, and you know it."

"I also know, sir, I do not have any authority whatever to assign any man to the job, whether he's rated for test pilot or not."

Marston got to his feet and refilled his coffee cup, and turned to face Brown. "I know what they say about me, all over Southeast Asia. That I'm easy. All a chopper's got to do is backfire once, and the pilot says he's not flying that death-trap pile of junk, and he crawls down off the seat and heads for the bar."

"You're a rated pilot, Marston."

"Without a medical. How do you think I got into this cruddy job?"

"You'll have a medical ten minutes from now, *if* . . . if you want it, and if you'll test fly the aircraft and stop letting these pilots refuse aircraft for *funny noises*."

"By God, let's go." Marston banged his coffee down so hard it slopped over on his desk. Thirty minutes later Doc Elmore had signed him off medically and Marston had on his hardhat, going up the ladder into the *Bell UH-1 "Huey Hog"* gunship, an aircraft that had been refused five times consecutively by five different pilots: Lieutenants Paulk and Gentel, Warrant Officers Woodley, Brandon, Edwards.

While Marston flew the ship over the base, putting it through all maneuvers and attitudes, Brown had the five pilots standing at attention before him, with Walker to one side, as rock-faced as his colonel. No one said a word. None of them moved, except Brown, who moved slowly around the ramp from time to time, smoking a cigar and studying the stolid pilots' faces. When the *Huey* began to lower and Marston put it into hover just above the ground for practice, holding it there, watching all the gauges, then Brown spoke. "I'll talk to you one at a time. You first, Paulk." Brown shot a look at Walker. "Have the others wait outside. They are not to discuss this among themselves. Put an MP standing over them if you think it necessary."

As Walker led the others out, there came the sound of the helicopter landing and shutting down. Walker returned, accompanied by Stavros, the clerk, who looked, walked and acted like a man instead of a queen. Brown had already solved that one, easily, by simply pulling Stavros aside and saying, "Prove it."

Stavros only shook his head, and then admitted, "No, sir, I'm not homosexual." He shrugged. "I just thought it might be a way to get out."

"There's only two ways out of here, kid. You do your year and then go home; or you leave earlier inside a mattress cover; and you're no hero either way. You're caught in the shit just like the rest of us."

"Yes, sir."

Brown sat down behind his desk, looked at Stavros in the other chair; the clerk nodded; Walker nodded also. Brown spoke and Stavros began taking shorthand:

"This is an informal inquiry into the reasons that 1/Lt Jack L. Paulk—get his service number and that stuff later, and the date of the refusal—Jack L. Paulk refused to fly

58

Bell helicopter UH dash One, number—get that off the a/c."

Brown looked up at Paulk. "This is not a courtmartial; it is only an inquiry, but if you wish to be represented by counsel we have one standing by."

"No, sir, I don't want a lawyer—at this time."

"Why did you refuse the aircraft, Paulk?"

Evidently Paulk was one of those ten-percenters: the guys who never seem to get the word or get it so late it does them little good. From the outset, it was obvious he had not gotten the full word on Colonel Joe Brown and intended shooting a line. He began by describing the kind of day it was, hot and humid, with a resulting high density altitude which made the air thin; then, as he began running up the engines for checkout, he could not achieve what he believed sufficient rpm to make flying safe under such conditions. He also mentioned, just in passing, that he was not personally feeling particularly well that day, little touch of the GIs, you know. . . .

Brown told Walker: "Check with the 509th and see how many missions they flew that day." Brown saw Paulk go pale. The 509th was stationed on the other side of this same helicopter base. "Also, check the medical records and see if Lieutenant Paulk made sick call on the day in question. Then check with Marston and have him dig out the aircraft records. See if Paulk signed a redline sheet, and what Marston's check of the complaint says."

Brown looked up at the white-faced 1/Lt. "Anything to add, Mr. Paulk?"

The lieutenant swallowed convulsively. "Sir, am I required to sign that statement?"

"I will ask you to sign it, after it's typed up in proper form."

"Sir— I, well, sir—"

"Yes, Paulk?"

"I guess I want to see that lawyer. . . ."

"You mean you lied?"

"No, sir, ah, well, not exactly."

"A not-exactly-lie is like a girl who isn't *quite* pregnant, Paulk. A fiction."

"I suppose so, sir. . . ."

"You want from under, Paulk?"

The man's whole posture changed as his face became eager and attentive. "Colonel, please, sir!"

"Get your ass out there, refuel that chopper, get a crew and fly me a mission. I don't care if you go shoot up a bunch of abandoned shithouses somewhere, but fly me a mission." Brown got to his feet and walked around the desk. "Paulk, if you refuse the aircraft now, it is an outright refusal to obey a lawful order from a superior officer under combat conditions."

"I'll fly it, sir," Paulk said, but it came hard.

"In case you change your mind, bring your lawyer when you come back to this office, Paulk. You haven't signed it, but we've got your so-called statement, and three witnesses, including myself. Dismissed."

The inquiries with the other four officer-pilots went in approximately the same fashion, except that Woodley, blond hair and blue eyes, kept alternating between a show of mild defiance and utter ass-kissing. He kept vacillating with however he thought the wind was blowing, trying to anticipate the colonel's wishes and what he thought the colonel might want him to say, until Brown told him, "Get your nose out of my bum and act as if you at least resemble a man." Then Woodley straightened up and told a story about fluctuating oil pressure when he ran up the engine, and he couldn't believe the gauge needle which rested in the green steady as a rock when he returned to the ramp. Then, he wanted to get confidential, give Colonel Brown the deep dope and inside-skinny on the 504 and all its ills. Brown heard him out for three minutes, then said, "Stavros, type up two statements for Mr. Woodley. One about his story on the airplane, the other concerning certain implied and insinuated accusations he has made against members of this command, which, if I remember correctly, include sodomy, drug addiction, smoking pot and various activities that could be classified as treasonable. And, oh yes, don't forget that about the black market activities."

Woodley's pale face went absolutely white as Stavros scribbled his shorthand notes, and Woodley finally managed to interject, "Oh, NO SIR! I didn't mean those as accusations, not at all. No, sir, I won't sign any statements against those men."

"What the hell were you, before you came out from under a rock and crawled over here with us?"

"I was a police cadet and helicopter-pilot trainee."

"It figures, you rumor-mongering motormouth." Brown looked at Woodley a moment longer, then said, "Get out of here!"

That afternoon, all five pilots flew the ship they had previously refused. During that time, Brown caught four hours sleep. When he woke, he wondered why his ulcer wasn't killing him, why he did not have to roll off his bunk and crawl to the sink and down a handful of chalky pills with a glass of water. Perhaps letting it all hang out was the best cure for an ulcer. Instead of keeping everything bottled up behind the facade of the cool, hard tough professional soldier, that tearing into this bunch of fools and incompetents in 504 was not only shaping up the unit but excellent therapy. Brown did not know; he was simply grateful.

He had finished showering, shaving, dressing, when Captain Walker knocked on the door, and, at command, entered. Brown took one glance at him and said, "Now what's the problem?"

"Saigon."

"March?"

"General Paulson himself."

"Any idea what it's about?"

"Everything would just about cover it."

"But the main pain?"

"Probably Kelley, sir. Those god damn CID men must have shot off their mouths an awful lot."

"In all my years in the army, Walker, I've never known men who could keep secrets more poorly, gossiped more, talked too much at the wrong time than the god damn CID. They go around whispering confidentially—in every god damn ear that will hold still long enough to listen, and every time they tell it, it always gets better, more elaborate, the details polished just a bit more. Key-rist!"

Walker nodded. He did not have the look of a happy young man. Brown thought he probably knew why, and said, "Doc Elmore finish his examinations?"

Walker nodded. "Yes, sir; about an hour ago."

"Results?"

"Incredible."

"God almighty. . . . All right, let's hear it."

"Thirty-five percent of the enlisted men are, or recently have been, users. There are twenty-one confirmed addicts, guys hooked through the balls and back again. Most of them are also pushers, to the other troops, the experimenters. I think 'joy-poppers' or some such word is the expression."

"And the officers?" Brown waited with an emptied out, hollowed-gut feeling that brought on the pain. He crammed in a handful of the pills and washed them down with water.

"Hopler was the only confirmed addict." Walker looked down at the floor. "Eight other officers are users; another fifteen have admitted occasional use of pot. All claim they have never flown after using."

"Which explains a hell of a lot of those aircraft refusals, doesn't it?"

"I'd say so, yes, sir. They know they'd be up to their asses in alligators if they removed themselves from flight status, grounded themselves for admitted use of marijuana, or any drug, so they do the obvious. Turn back the ships, for alleged malfunctions. The pilots and crewmen who don't monkey with drugs at all figure, 'What the hell? Why go risk my ass when Hopler won't fly because he's stoned!' So they turn back the choppers. It's like back pains. . . . Who the hell can prove you wrong?"

"By God I can make the effort. The very first thing is seal this base. Run every Viet on the place right out through the front gate. Double, triple, whatever you have to do, have the guards hold hands if you must, but seal off this base. Then get some of those god damn mouthy CID men in here to see if any of our people are growing their own marijuana, or if some smart kid with a couple years chemistry has got him a heroin plant going. Get on the phone first and make an appointment with Elmore; tell him I'm coming over for my flight physical. Soon as I get that, you're giving me a check ride so I can get current; then—"

"Pardon me, Colonel, but what about General Paulson?"

"We've just had a communications breakdown."

Walker grinned, saluted, bolted through the door in a run. A moment later he returned, sheepishly, dialed the flight surgeon, made the appointment, and ran out again.

Elmore said, "Read that chart on the wall . . . any line you may have memorized will do," and laughed. Brown stood across the room and read the 20/15 line, then pulled out his glasses and read the fine print on the card Elmore handed him. "How's your blood pressure?"

"High right now because I've got the ass."

"Critical?"

"Hell, no."

"Anything else wrong with you?"

"Ulcer."

"Incapacitating?"

"Of course not."

"Excellent." Elmore made some checks on the forms, signed a portion of it inter-leaved with several carbons, tore off the top, original, copy and handed it over. "Have a nice flight, Colonel."

"Thanks."

"Next!" Another man came through the door as Brown left. As he walked toward the flight line Brown saw the 504 guard personnel, assisted by MPs, herding the Viets toward the main gate. Walker waited beside the same ship that had been used all day by the other pilots who'd once refused it. They climbed in and Walker gave Brown an hour's checkride and signed off his logbook. As the sun started down, they went up again, and Brown qualified for night flight, as required: the airborne maneuvers, liftoffs and landings. At nine o'clock that night, Brown led 504, personally, on the first mission against an armed enemy that the unit had flown in more than seven weeks. Six gunships went out on the mission. Four returned to base.

7

The mission call came in from an *FAC* (a forward air controller flying a small single engine Cessna) over the *U Minh Forest* in the delta. It is a place of such vast dimensions and such thick, jungly growth that it had become the major VC sanctuary in the south. A labyrinth of vines, giant trees, tall grass, deadly snakes and stalking tigers that took men like any other fair game.

The substance of the *FAC*'s frantic call was that a company of slick ships, lightly armed troop-carrying helicopters, had put down a unit of *ARVN* troops in the *U Minh*, and the South Vietnamese troops were, as customary, either running away and deserting to the VC, or getting the shit kicked out of them if they fought.

Brown called a hurried briefing of all flight personnel, stood on the platform and told them, "You all have copies of the new crew assignments. We're taking six ships. I'm leading, Walker's riding tail-end Charlie. The other five aircraft commanders are Lieutenants Paulk and Gentel, Warrants Bass, Brandon and Edwards." Brown shot a look at Woodley, and the warrant officer looked like a man just given a reprieve as the phone rang while they strapped him into an electric chair. Brown had a passing thought. He has to go, that gossipy yellow trash.

Brown said, "Aircraft commanders, find your men and be on the line in ten minutes, and I don't want any god damn standing around like airline pilots with this bullshit attitude of all I do is fly the bloody thing. Help the armorers and get yourselves ready. Any of you with death wishes, who like to be showoffs, or think you are John Wayne, forget it. Every man wears his hardhat and flak vest, survival kit and personal sidearm. One thing: a lot of you people walking around with these odd-ball weapons, get rid of them—those *Swedish K* automatic pistols, the captured gook stuff. You're going to get your asses shot off some day because you ran out of ammo in a tight spot. Get the weapons that were issued to you, and a unit of fire for each. Let's go!"

They took off through a low overcast and Brown was almost immediately on instruments, but the layer was thin and he came through on top and saw the stars as he made his turn toward the target area, what the French call *la foret de la nuit,* the forest of darkness.

Brown made a slow S-turn, left, then back right and on course, saw the five other ships formed up behind him, red rotating beacons sending flashes through the night sky. Brown turned his combat radio to the *FAC* frequency and heard the young pilot's voice. They were a breed apart, the *FAC*s, mostly young, some very young, warrant officers, a few lieutenants. Because of the danger they endured daily, sometimes flying ten hours a day, stopping just long enough to refuel, rearm, eat a sandwich, they were absolutely savage in their hatred for the Viet Cong and North Vietnamese. The "armament" of the *FAC* airplanes consisted of four small rockets mounted on wing pods, two on each wing; and the personal weapon, revolver or .45 Colt automatic pistol strapped around the pilot's waist. The VC felt about *FAC* the way a man under indictment feels toward his accuser, the guy who put the finger on him. *FAC*s knew if they went down they would live only as long as they could outrun Charley, or empty his handgun into the VC surrounding him. Charley took no *FAC* prisoners. Sometimes the Charley skinned captured *FAC*s alive, staked them down over ant-beds, or emasculated them and stuffed their genitals into their mouths.

Charley also did the same to gunship crewmen, if they were captured. But the "Hog" airmen were a good deal harder to capture. Each *Bell UH-1 "Huey Hog"* gunship was armed with four fixed 7.62mm machineguns, two more identical machineguns mounted on flexible mounts that were manned by the door-gunners. Also mounted on each side of the fuselage were multiple pods firing *2.75 HVAR* rockets, and then a little, tricky thing called the *Emm-Fiver* (M-5) which automatically hurled 40mm grenades wherever aimed by the pilot, who in the Hog is also the fire controller—the main gunner, just as on a fighter plane.

When Brown heard the FAC's voice on the radio FAC was speaking to a calm and controlled, but fear-constricted, voice to the airborne controller of the operation, so Brown switched radio frequencies to the controller, thumbed his microphone and said, "Markdown, this is the Downhill Gang: Do you read, over?"

Markdown answered instantly. "Christ, I hope you guys are coming fullballs, Downhill. We've got problems. Those poor guys are getting the shit shot out of them."

"Rog, Markdown, throttles against the stops, estimate reaching you in seven minutes."

"There may be nothing left but disintegrated human garbage by then."

All Brown replied was, "Rog," knowing the man knew the capabilities of the Hogs.

A few minutes later Markdown said, "Downhill, I have contact, see your flashers . . . FAC, fire smoke . . . Downhill, watch for FAC's white phosphorous, then bore in and see if you can take some of the heat off those guys."

"Rog, Markdown. Where are the slicks to pick up what's left? We don't want any goddam mid-airs up here tonight."

Voice dripping contempt, controller said, "Those sons of bitches are about seven miles west of here, either hoping to run short of fuel or God to come down and deliver them back to the pilots' bar."

"Rog, Controller, contact." Brown thumbed another button and spoke to his flight. "I have contact visually with the FAC's smoke rocket, and I see muzzle-flashes from ground fire. I'm turning on my searchlight and going down to draw their fire and take out what I can. Follow me in. Captain Walker, you ride in tail-end Charley and shoot down any Downhill Gang ship that tries to break off without making his run."

Walker replied laconically, "Rog, will do . . . gladly."

Brown had forgotten about the noise.

Almost the instant he turned on his searchlight his ship became a target. The muzzle-flashes turned upward toward him, instead of being tiny and short as they appeared when firing level and seen from above. One of the first shots went through the plastic windshield ten inches from his face. He flinched and felt a looseness around the lower parts of his body but it was like that first punch when he used to fight; it turned on a switch inside of him and he wanted to kill his opponent. He spotted a target, ruddered around to aim at it, and let loose, just as his doorgunners also began firing.

Brown had forgotten the noise.

After he crawled back inside his skin he was all right; but, for a moment, he thought the entire ship had exploded around him and he, somehow, kept on riding a padded chair through space.

But in a half-minute he was back into it, the way he got back into it when he had the first fight after a lay-off, and he poured machine gun and rocket fire into the VC positions surrounding the entrapped ARVN troops. Brown was down almost on the deck now. In the searchlight he could see the slack bodies of dead and wounded and the upturned faces of other ARVN troops, some curled into tiny fetal humps and, doubtlessly, calling for mother. As Brown pulled up and peeled off to his right he looked back over his shoulder, as he let the ship come on around and he saw Number Two, piloted by Paulk, break off and make a ninety degree turn, going low and fast across the top of the trees. The son of a bitch just did not want any of it. Brown let his ship drift sideways as he climbed so he could watch the others make their runs. Gentel went all the way through, but high and too fast and both the rockets he fired overshot by a hundred yards, bursting harmlessly in the jungle far beyond the VC that had the ARVN troops trapped.

Brown said into his radio, "Downhill Three, you yellow prick. You'd better put it *in* there next run or your ass is mine!"

"Downhill Three, sir, I thought I saw—"

"You lying shit, get off the air!"

Brandon went in, all the way in. Perhaps, he was shot through the head by ground fire, became hypnotized by fear or his depth-perception failed him; or he got a visual fixation on his instrument panel or even had his eyes closed. He crashed in a huge, gushing blossom of fire, fortunately beyond the encircled ARVNs and maybe he killed a few Charleys as well as his crew, himself and an aircraft.

Edwards didn't even try. He made a shallow run, then pulled off, and started calling MAYDAY on his radio, claiming he'd taken ground fire through the engine, that his oil pressure was bouncing like a yo-yo and his engine surging and he was heading back to base. He never got there. He landed at another base, and Brown learned later that the instant the rotorblades on the Hog stopped turning, Edwards went up the side of the ship like a baboon and stayed there for a half-hour, doing something with—or to—the engine. He refused to allow his crew or any of the base mechanics to assist him.

Walker made the kind of run that Brown had made with his searchlight on, boring in 'till he skimmed across the clearing; got a secondary explosion out of something in the forest beyond the line of VC troops, probably an ammo dump, and tore hell out of his Hog, flying through the debris as he pulled up.

They made two more runs while the slicks came in to get the troops out. In order to make Gentel land his Hog and let the doorgunners put their machineguns to work directly into the VC, Brown had to ride over the top of Gentel's ship and threaten to come down on him and collide in midair. Once Gentel was down, Brown rode around toward the far side and put down. Walker was already on the ground, pouring it in, lifting up time-to-time, to hover and shift his position so he could bring his fixed guns to bear on new targets, as Brown did. Paulk had disappeared and Brown could not raise him on the radio.

Once the slicks came in they simply made passes, few of them landing, but hovering, while as many able men as possible jumped aboard and helped what wounded they could. One which did land was blown to pieces by an AK-47 from the VC line and this so discouraged the rest of the Vietnamese slickship pilots that they shoved off for home. Brown did not know and he never found out, how many live and wounded of their own the Viet slickship pilots left abandoned on the battlefield. He did know that one of his own gunners, Pat Beach, jumped out of Brown's Hog and pulled three wounded Viets aboard and found room for another two live ones to ride, before Brown saw it was useless to remain longer, and radioed Walker and Gentel as he lifted off, "Downhill Gang, let's get out of this clipjoint."

As the ships neared base, Brown heard Walker's laconic voice, "Another ship's joining up on us, starboard aft."

Brown already knew, but he asked, "Paulk?"

"Rog."

Brown landed first, then Gentel, followed by Paulk; Walker last, herding them home.

Brown waited beside Paulk's ship as it shut down, and stood facing the red-haired pilot when the man climbed through the door, grinning and shaking his head, "I swear, that's the first time in my *life* I ever got lost!"

One of Paulk's doorgunners turned his head and spit, viciously; and then he walked away, heels driving hard against the concrete ramp under his feet.

Brown did not say anything to Paulk. He stared at the man until the grin faded and the lips pinched up in fear, and he looked away, past Brown's shoulder, down some long tunnel; perhaps toward the day he could tell that lie often enough so he could come to believe it himself.

"Mr. Paulk, I will remind you that a debriefing interrogation following a mission is a sworn statement. It must be verified by your crewmen, other airmen in the same action, and signed by you. I do not know the penalty for willful perjury, but I'm sure the 504th's law officer could enlighten you upon the subject."

Naturally, the others had gathered around. Brown shot a look at Gentel; the tubby pilot was grinning widely and his hands were in motion, the way pilots' hands often are when talking about flying. Gentel had his tubby gut sucked in as much as he could and his broad shoulders squared back; and he was telling them all about it, ground engineers, other crewmen; he had completely forgotten what it had taken to force him to make his runs and get him on the ground at the landing zone. Brown looked on past Gentel and saw that on the side of Gentel's Huey was painted *Saigon Suzie*, and a naked girl with enormous breasts. Brown made a mental note for the maintenance officer, but just then Marston came up, concern and real compassion making lines on his face. "Lost two, sir?"

Brown nodded. "Brandon went in. But Edwards called a MAYDAY, groundfire through the engine, losing oil pressure—" He did not finish; Marston knew the symptoms better than Brown did. "He may have made it down some place," Marston said, hopefully. "Maybe he'll call in."

Brown nodded again, vaguely. Once more he found himself looking at *Saigon Suzie* and the tits. He turned to Marston, and as he did so, Brown drew out his pocket notebook and a pencil. He found a blank page and on it he drew:

$$\frac{O\,O}{MM}$$

He tore out the page and gave it to Marston. "Tonight, paint out all this cute air force Hollywood horseshit," he pointed at Gentel's chopper, "on all 504 aircraft. Then put this mark on the nose and on each side of every Hog."

Marston took the paper, looked at it, turned it upside down, righted it and looked at Brown. "Sir, may I ask what it is?"

71

"That there is my old granddad's cattle brand. He used it on a ranch he once had down in Mexico."

"Yes, sir. . . . Ah, Colonel, ah, what does it stand for?"

"Two mummified assholes on a bar. It is the brand of the downhill gang. And the Downhill Gang is *us*!" Brown stared around the men who stood watching him in the gloom of the dim nightlights on the ramp. "Until we start coming up the other side."

He turned and strode away, Walker at his side, voice urgent as he spoke. "Stavros got word out to the line and one of the mechanics told me. They're waiting for you in your office."

"March?"

"Shit, no, Colonel. General Paulson himself." Walker touched Brown's hand. "I guess we'd better get cleaned up first, huh, sir?"

"Hell, no! We're going right on in as we are. Let the bastard see and have a nose full of what this war looks like and smells like. Come on!"

8

Brown was perfectly aware that he was playing a role when he strode into his office still dressed in grimy flight suit, hardhat, sweat-soaked leather flying gloves and scuffed boots; and emanating the stink of hoglike body odor, cordite, and blood off the wounded ARVNs Pat Beach had managed to save on the landing zone. And he readily admitted that he liked the contrast that his appearance made with that of General Paulson, who stood in sharply creased summer-weight khaki gabardines, polished paratroop boots (which he was not entitled to wear because he'd never been through jump school) and a large cigar jutting from his mouth. The imitation, or emulation, did not carry over. Wallace Paulson could make the effort and play the role the rest of his life, but nobody on earth would ever mistake him for Curtis LeMay.

To Arizona-born, ranch-raised Joe Brown General Paulson was like a drugstore cowboy. He wore the clothes, but his boots were run over at the heels and of obviously cheap manufacture, his jeans were just a little too short and showed lots of wear on the butt, but none inside each thigh. His hat fit too high on his head and the crown had those cow-milker creases front and rear, indicating that rather than riding a horse and punching cattle, he'd had his head buried up in the flank of some old Jersey cow, pulling on her teats.

Joe Brown had known Wallace Paulson since they were classmates at the Point. At one time they had known one another extremely well, when Paulson made the weight and went after Joe Brown's captaincy of the boxing team; and Joe Brown knocked Wallace Paulson out in one minute and nine seconds of the first round. Paulson was not able to bear that, he being a first-classman and Joe Brown only a third-classman—sophomore. So Paulson dropped out of the boxing squad and went on to other pursuits his senior year. After Joe Brown's graduation from the Academy, and especially after becoming a pilot, he and Paulson had crossed tracks frequently. After the Air Force was made a separate entity army aviation became, and is, a rather small and, somewhat, intimate community. There just aren't so many of them that most army pilots don't know one another, if not personally, then almost certainly by reputation. Until he made eagle colonel, Paulson's reputation was that of an adequate and ultra-conservative pilot. His philosophy, not original with him, was: "If my ass gets there safe, then the passengers got nothing to worry about." Nobody could safely argue with this outlook, unless he wished to be answered by the other old, extremely unoriginal response:

"There are old pilots,
And there are bold pilots;
But there are *no* old bold pilots."

Which was fine, except that Paulson carried his attitude toward aviation safety like a shield of the One True Faith. Naturally, he developed a reputation. There were many officers who might go so far as to delay a trip in order to fly with Paulson, and there were others who believed that as a career army pilot Paulson had hired out to fly when the flying needed doing. Paulson courted the first group, gave the captive audience lectures while in the air. The word for what he did, and what he became, the reputation he finally earned for himself was, quite simply, a kissass. He made colonel ahead of his number, and general far earlier than most of his contemporaries, some of whom were extremely more qualified. And, then, as predictably as drought on a ranch without irrigation wells, once he became general, Paulson became a virtual fire-eater. He chomped cigars, "helled" and "god damned" around the place, particularly in mixed company, didn't know what the god damn country was coming to, the gutless wonders training command turned out wearing wings

74

nowadays, and he posed beautifully for photographs. He was posing now, except there was no cameraman. Joe Brown supposed the pose was to frighten him, to make him believe that Paulson had come to tear strips off Joe Brown's hide. Brown could hardly keep from laughing, with contempt. For despite Paulson's well-earned reputation over the years as a suckup, Brown had never been able to think of Paulson in any other way than as a quitter, as a man who believed when it got too tough to cut it was time to leave. He was the kind of man who'd make one attempt at a rugged instrument landing approach, miss it, haul ass for the alternate airport, and then accuse a pilot who did shoot the approach, and make it, of violating the minimum ceiling regulations.

Just by looking at Paulson, Joe Brown knew why Paulson was here, and Joe Brown thought, the son of a bitch is going to screw me.

Paulson shot a look at Walker and said, "You're dismissed for the time being, young man."

Walker did not move, except to turn his head and see what Colonel Brown had to say about that. Paulson said, "You don't need confirmation from Colonel Brown, Captain. I'm ranking officer here."

Brown jerked his chin toward the door and Walker left, making his reluctance obvious, so much so that Brown knew Walker would be right outside the door, and doubtlessly listening to every word.

The door closed behind Walker and Paulson shouted, "Would you mind telling me what in the *hell* is going on down here?" Before Brown could answer, Paulson stuck up his left hand, fingers spread, and began counting off: "First, I get a report that you physically assaulted two subordinates at *Tan Son Nhut*, before ever taking active command of 504. Broke one's jaw, for Christ's sake, an enlisted man. Then, you charge another EM, a black, for God's sake—and you know how sensitive *that* is—and then you pick up a deadly weapon, a *grenade*, and throw it with such force the blow hospitalizes the man you struck with it."

75

Paulson stopped for air, shaking his head. "You use filthy language, insulting and degrading, to officer and enlisted man alike; you have placed at least two men under arrest, including two officers; you ran narcotics urine tests without authority—that'll be all over the god damn wire services and Stateside TV tomorrow! You assaulted a whole building full of messcooks with a firehose; you've fired your adjutant and flight surgeon; you *may*—I don't know because the CID hasn't filed a full report—but you *may* be about to face some kind of manslaughter or other homicide charge, regarding Kelley."

Paulson stopped, shook his head, looked around the room, threw the spitty cigar butt into a can, then shouted, "Well, haven't you anything to say?"

"I have."

"All right, let's hear it."

"Your fucking informer, whoever he is, forgot to tell you one other thing. This outfit flew a successful mission tonight. The first in seven god damn weeks. I've been here just about twenty-four hours, and this rotten, cruddy, stoned outfit has shaped up enough to fly a fucking mission."

Paulson's face was red, his throat worked, and his hand came up, finger pointing at Brown, jerking, as he tried to shout and Brown yelled right back into his face. "Or wasn't that what I was sent down here for? To put the busher outfit back into the war?"

Paulson finally got his voice working again; he was so angry he had to sit down and hold his chest; and his voice was astonishingly quiet. He panted for a moment, then said, "You're through, Brown. Through. I'll have you up on so many charges—You can't talk to me like that. I swear, you're through."

Brown said, "That's the best news I've heard since the day I got that lousy god damn letter back home in Arizona."

Brown stepped to the door and jerked it open, and shouted, "Captain Walker, get the MPs at once. I have just been placed under arrest by General Paulson."

76

Paulson reared up from his chair. "NO! *Wait!*"

Walker came to stand in the door, and Paulson looked at him, head cocked to one side, curiously, and then he said in a voice unlike him in every way, uncertain: "Walker? Captain Dale L. Walker?"

Walker saluted and said, "Yes, sir."

"But—" Paulson looked up at Brown, and Brown fastened two cold, marble-hard, green eyes on him. The general looked back to Walker and in a subdued voice, he said, "But aren't you one of those—I mean—at *Tan Son Nhut*? . . .

Without blinking, Walker said, "I don't believe I know to what the general is referring, sir."

Paulson fumbled open a shirt pocket and took out a small custom-made silver-backed notepad. He opened it, looked at Walker and read off a serial number, and Walker said, "Yes, that is my service number."

Paulson sighed, as deeply as a man who has just rolled off his wife after one of the greatest climaxes. He let himself fall back into the chair as though boneless, and after a moment lifted a hand, and said quietly, "Please close the door."

Paulson's posture was not that of a general officer on a mission of hatchet-wielding. He looked more like a drugstore cowboy with his "spurs" caught in a barstool. Apparently, Paulson became aware of his appearance and he assumed the proper posture of a West Point graduate while sitting down: his back was straight as the leading edge of a fixed-wing aircraft, head up, elbows on the desk, fingers interlaced, his thumbs pushing up under the point of his chin. Paulson sighed again, this time with apparent weariness, and said, "Tell me."

They told him, Walker contributing where it seemed that his offering would further explain, or elaborate; but Brown told the story and he told it straight, withholding nothing. And when he finished, Brown made a demand: "Either get your informer out of my command, General Paulson, or relieve me of my command. If you refuse to do either, I herewith submit, orally, my resignation from the United States Army."

"My *God*, Joe!"

"I won't have a backshooter, General, running the ridges behind me and smuggling out incomplete reports about me, my men, my unit, my activities."

"All right, Joe."

"I will do you the courtesy of not asking his identity."

"Thank you."

"I'll just tell you who, if you don't mind."

Paulson sighed deeply and shook his head, still holding the rigid thumbs under his chin.

"Major Bertram Wright came to you first, and then someone he left behind has kept the reports coming in. I'd say it was the buttfaced assistant flight surgeon Wright had climbing walls." Brown turned to Walker. "What's his name?"

"Wagnon, Gregory Wagnon."

Paulson said, "I'll take him out with me tonight."

"Let him stay if you wish. We might teach him something about aviation, and other things."

Paulson looked up at Brown with genuine puzzlement. Brown said, "Of course you've read Saint-Exupery?"

General Paulson nodded.

"Wind, Sand and Stars?"

"Of course."

"There is a sentence in that book it might not hurt Wagnon to learn, and to understand: *'To be a man is, precisely, to be responsible.'* That what life is *not* all about is deals, conning, working others, conniving others to work for you." Brown laughed. "We might even make a man of the sneaky son of a bitch. If Elmore gets time to sink hooks into him, I guarantee it."

Paulson nodded, and said, "All right, Joe. But the CID has its behind clear up over its shoulders, over what happened at the messhall and the EM club this morning."

Brown walked to the desk and put his hands down on it, leaning very close to General Paulson. "Fuck CID, Wally. That's an ugly, filthy, rotten and inexcusable word

78

for officers of our training, breeding, character and experience to use; but I say it again. Double and with handles on. Do you think for one single moment that if CID, CIC *and* that utterly ridiculous CIA did their work properly, the graft and corruption and deviousness of all Vietnam would be anywhere near the level it is today? Christ, General, the Orientals, and the Arabs are supposed to be the world's masters at deception, intrigue, all that crud; but we've got guys that teach the Viets new tricks."

"Now, Joe—"

"This is my *fifth*—say again! This is my *fifth* tour of duty in this shithole. I didn't spend four of those years lying on my butt in bed or flying missions. I was not married in those days. I got around. You know who the best pimp in the whole delta area was two years ago? Boyd Rogers. . . . I see, General, the name is familiar to you. That's right, Boyd Rogers, chief of CID in the Mekong. He could furnish *anything*: a Negro airline stew from the Congo, a red-haired Peace Corps volunteer from the Philippines, with incredible tits; any kind or color shade of Viet, or if a guy liked boys . . . any age. . . ."

Brown pulled up the other chair in the room and sat down across the desk from Paulson. "General, I did not want this job, I don't like it and I'll turn it back to you the instant you'll relieve me. I want to go home. I want to be with my bride." Then Brown's voice took on the tone and edge of the shrapnel from a Claymore mine. "But so long as I command this unit, I *command*. You can take that, or leave it . . . or shove it up your ass!"

Brown got to his feet, kicking the chair aside and stood hands on hips, ready. For a long, stretched-out moment that kept on lengthening so Walker could not keep still. General Paulson said nothing. Then he got slowly to his feet, looked around the room vaguely, almost as though not completely aware of where he was, exactly what had happened or was about to happen, to him. Then he reached down. Brown could see him reach for it, in the shape of Paulson's trained body, the posture of his back, the almost visible reaction of his mind. Then Paulson

79

reached down and got hold of what he was, brought it to the surface, and once more became the man everyone knew—the cigar chomper, the brittle-eyed, jut-jawed, immaculate, hard-nosed, cursing general . . . posing for his god damn photograph.

Brown was almost choking with disappointment, until Paulson said, just exactly like Frank Lovejoy portraying General LeMay in the movies, "OK, Brown; you've got some small problems. They don't interest me. Results are all that count!"

Brown thought to himself, if I were June Allyson, I'd skip across the room and kiss the son of a bitch!

Paulson jerked the door open and strode out, leaving the door open. In wonderment, Walker stood and looked at Joe Brown, and without asking permission he sat down in the chair that Brown had kicked across the room. Brown looked at him and grinned. "Your face is hanging out, Captain."

"Shit, man—I mean, Colonel, sir—now I *know* what that tired old phrase means: *command presence*. Christ, you've *got* it! I know what the other phrase means, keeping control of the situation. A colonel and a general. . . ." Walker's voice was husky with awe. "You played that phoney son of a bitch like a five-string banjo, *Bonaparte's Retreat*. . . ."

"That's a terrible way to talk about a general officer of the United States Army."

Walker shot to his feet and bowed deeply from the waist, saying, "I beg most earnestly the Colonel's excusal of my disrespectful remark."

Then he straightened and grinned like an old housepet pussy cat who'd finally captured, frightened to death and eaten, with relish, the pet goldfish.

Brown laughed aloud. Then he said with deadly calm, "Get that Assistant FS, Wagnon, in here. Then check the chow halls, detail someone you trust to make an inspection of the line guarding the camp, find out when Marston can have that junker of yours flying again, bring me Paulk's debriefing interrogation report and those of his crewmen. Then arrange for the MPs to bring Hopler to me for an interview at oh-eight-hundred; and fix it so the shithead's got a lawyer with him so there won't be any delays. Tell Stavros I want something to eat and a pot of coffee, put through a recommendation for the Distinguished Service Cross for Pat Beach; work up some letters for the families of Brandon and his crewmen, and get someone to go through their gear, very carefully! So we don't send momma any condoms or blowjob photos. Try to find out what happened to Edwards; he went down or made some other base safely, whatever—You getting all this?"

"I'm catching on, Colonel."

"Meaning?"

"I'm with you so constantly I know a lot of what has to be done without orders."

"How do you like your new job?"

"Gangbusters, man, gangbusters. I sure don't have any trouble getting to sleep, when I get near my bunk!"

"Like I told you, sonny; you got to learn to sleep in the wintertime."

Walker looked at him curiously.

Tired clear through to his bone marrow, Brown managed to grin, and said, "Sorry, that's something an old cowpuncher told me once."

"I understand, sir. We sleep after the work's all done, right?"

"I hope every airline turns you down!"

Walker laughed, and asked, "What else, sir?"

"You tell me."

"Mission report, your own interrogation debriefing. The conduct of those ARVN slickship pilots, the slope chickenshits! Make a real pilot puke. Also—"

"Screw it," Brown said, so tired and used up he seemed to see Walker through the wrong end of a telescope, so Walker appeared a thousand meters distant though his voice was close and clear. "We catch it next time it comes up."

"Yes, sir," Walker said, saluting smartly. In a friendly

but not familiar voice, Walker said, "Get some rest, sir. Goodnight."

Brown stumbled to his bunk, and became aware he'd not stopped playing the role for Paulson; he still wore his flight helmet, his suit, even his gloves. At the bunk in the corner of the office, he turned and sat down. He managed to get the hardhat off, and his gloves, to unzip his flight suit to his waist and unlace one boot, when sleep took him and perhaps, saved his life.

Sometime during the night, someone fragged Colonel Joe Brown. He was so exhausted, and nearly fully clothed, he hardly even became aware of the pain. He only knew he had been fragged and wounded when he awoke next morning in hospital. On the bed next to him lay Warrant Officer Hopler, the drug addict; and across the aisle with his wired-up broken jaw, Sergeant Travis Charles sat on his bunk sucking soup through a glass straw, with hatred in his dark eyes.

Brown looked around. Farther on down the ward lay the displayer of the MAT 50 the day of Brown's arrival, the one he'd given the three-quarter overhand fastball shot with the grenade. Nice to be among old friends.

Brown shifted his body, and he felt something solid and metallic and familiar just under the small of his back, on the left side. Cautiously, he slipped his hand under the sheet, and he felt the familiar snug fit in his hand of his .45 Colt automatic pistol. He let his fingers rove over it, to see how it was, and it was just exactly right, as he'd have done it himself—the .45 was cocked, which indicated a round in the chamber, the thumb safety on. All Brown had to do to defend himself was raise the big pistol up, grip it, move his left index finger down, because he was left-handed, not right-handed, flick the safety off, and he was in business. He looked at his watch; it was almost eight o'clock in the morning. Time for an interview with Wagnon. Brown reached for the buzzer to call the nurse, or medic, whichever appeared.

9

Brown's wounds were not critical. Once the wardchief answered the buzzer summons and discovered it was Colonel Brown who rang, he went for Doc Elmore. Elmore came striding down the open space between the rows of bunks and stopped, his slightly pock-marked face in a wide grin. "Made it home alive once more, eh, Chief?"

Elmore was not a disrespectful man, nor was he given to untoward familiarity concerning superior officers. It was simply that Elmore was a man who had the sense to place proper value upon himself, his training and his skills, his experience, dignity and personal integrity; and he demanded that others value him equally in, or outside, the army. He called Colonel Brown "Chief" because it was not only a title of respect like "Skipper," but because he was also aware of Brown's American Indian ancestry, which showed in the lean, long-muscled body, the tilted green eyes.

"On a guess, I'd say I got fragged," Brown said.

"Not a bad guess for a man full of various medication, some of which is supposed to make him sleep, not confer."

"How bad am I?"

"Bad enough. Most of it took you in the back, four nice splinters; almost as though you'd been stabbed. But your old redskin luck held. Your right lung should have a hole in it, but the splinter slowed down enough coming through all that meat and bone so it only bruised your lung." Elmore raised a finger and waggled it twice. "No smoking. Absolutely none."

"Can I work?"

"Not yet." And Brown did not like the look on Elmore's face. He asked, "What haven't you told me?"

"After some of the medication wears off, you are going to have a very peculiar feeling inside, a heaviness, like all your insides are filled with trembling jelly. Your body cavity is full of blood and we've got to get it out."

"That means opening me up very wide, like enough for a scoop shovel, to clean me out."

Elmore nodded. "We've given you four transfusions already, but there's a leak in there some place and we have to get inside, Chief, clean out the old stuff and plug the hole."

"When can you start?"

"I think you should go out for it, perhaps to the big hospital in Japan, or even Stateside."

"You can't do the job?"

"I can do it, but this isn't the place for it."

"Why?"

"Limited facilities, for one thing; only two men I can really depend upon for another; and——"

"And I'd be helpless. . . ."

Elmore took a deep breath, moved a bit closer and lowered his voice. "You'd be out of it for a day, perhaps two days, simply too weak and drugged so that even that old pistola Walker slipped under your sheet . . . you wouldn't have the strength to lift it."

"But after that?"

"Joe, I'd like to take care of that ulcer while I'm in there."

"Say you did that, too," and Brown was grateful to hear Elmore say *I* because it meant the doctor had probably allowed himself to decide he would do the job himself.

Elmore said, "I can't make any guarantees; I'm not eager to make any guesses." Elmore looked around, then stepped away from the bed, got a chair and brought it back, sat down and leaned close to Brown. "Look, Joe, this is your chance to get the hell *out*. I can, and I damned sure will, with complete integrity, write up a report, diag-

84

nosis and prognosis, that in three days time will put you flat on your back, Stateside. How about it?"

For a long time, Joe Brown did not say anything, but the thought came to his mind, at once, when Elmore made the offer, and Brown finally told him the thought. "I don't like not finishing things once I start them."

"Joe—"

"Let me think on it. How fast do we have to move?"

"Now." Elmore raised his arm and looked at his watch. "I'll be back in ten minutes. That's all I can give you. We've got to get that coagulated blood out of your body cavity. In ten minutes, we either put you aboard the 'Dustoff' chopper standing by, or we prep you for the surgery here."

"All right, do the surgery here, the swabbing out. I can decide the other later."

"You're a fool, Joe. This is your chance to go out. They wouldn't dare send you back. Go home to your wife, Joe, god damn it *go home!*"

Brown closed his eyes and said, "Let me have my ten minutes." Joe heard Elmore's muttering curses and footsteps fading. All his mind saw was the shape of Jody's face looking at him in that way of hers, that all-in-one expression showing him love, respect, desire and—faith. And he kept hearing her say, *"You don't know how not to do your job. You've never had any practice."*

Brown reached for the button and a moment later he saw Elmore hurrying toward the bed where he lay. As the doctor halted at the foot of the bed, an expectant smile on his lips, Brown said, "The surgery, doc. Let's get it on."

"God damn you." Elmore shook his head, then lowered his face and wiped his eyes. He turned away, muttering, "Stubborn god damn redskin!"

Brown woke the first time in a foul-tasting haze of pain and the feel of bindings all about his upper body. He vaguely saw Wagnon sitting in a chair beside the bed; and all the tubes, bottles and junk and he faded out again, thinking, god damn I'd like to brush my teeth. . . .

Brown came back all the way the second time he woke and he was not quite sure he believed how much pain his body seemed to be making an effort to endure. Brown had known for a long time the old fiction about how God had been kind to men and had given them a built-in mechanism that would make them automatically lapse into unconsciousness if a pain became more than they could bear. What men did when hit by pain they could not bear was cry for their mothers or curse till their throats stopped working; they shit their pants and wet all over themselves. Probably, some of them prayed or recited their beads, although Brown had never seen a man in that kind of pain praying or holding a rosary; and possibly, men in that kind of pain did other things Brown had never seen or had someone tell him about. There was just the one thing Brown was sure of: there was no God-installed automatic device that made men pass out when pain became unendurable.

So it was with this knowledge that Brown took his pain and made his fight, step by step, like going up a ladder. He fought it, and once he had some handles on it and seemed to be holding it in a place where he could stand it, Brown told himself: "It can't get any worse."

But the pain was not paying any attention to Joe Brown. Pain was an inexorably moving machine like a steamroller driven by a robot. It kept coming at Joe Brown, tearing the temporary handles from his hands so he had to grapple and fight with it again, till he had hold of it and saw a sliver of daylight and got a single, good, deep breath of air; and, then, that goddam robot let in the clutch of the steamroller again and made a liar out of Joe Brown, each time he said, "It can't get any worse than this. . . ."

By the time Elmore found Joe Brown, Brown was actually climbing the wall; because in his fight against the pain he had discovered that, if he moved his body in a certain way, reaching upward with a slight twist of his chest toward the wall beside his bed, it seemed to give him a handle he could hold on to longer.

Elmore took one single look, then turned and ran. In fifteen seconds he was back, with the syringe in his hand, and he gave Joe Brown a jolt that brought him down off the wall and put him to sleep and away from the robot-driven steamroller.

And then Elmore turned to the white-faced man beside him. In a voice that kept choking with emotion and anger, Elmore told Wagnon: "We knew you were a snitch for Wright, for Saigon. We did not know you were an assassin."

"Now listen here, Major—"

"You listen. At this moment, that man might die. Because of your neglect. Are you listening to me, do you read me, loud and clear, five-by-five?"

"Yes, sir."

"If Colonel Brown dies, of shock induced by the pain which arose entirely because of your neglect, I will not only see that you never practice medicine again, I will do everything within my power to see that you are brought to trial on charges of willful murder."

Wagnon's eyes were the size of brown jarlids, and his girlish mouth worked without sound, until he finally panted, "Sir, you can't be serious!"

"Serious? I have just stated to you, young man—no, *man* is a misnomer as applied to you, and you have proved to me you are *not* a doctor for both those imply responsibility, which you have, likewise, proved you lack."

"Sir, I—"

"Shut up, you—you *informer*, you self-serving, ambitious, kissassy *informer* and liar."

Virtually consumed by his emotion, Elmore's hand shot out and his fist gripped a handful of Wagnon's white smock. He pulled the younger doctor to him so they stood face to face, chests touching. "I made you a *promise*. You dig that, baby? You and your jive talk around the hospital, in the wards. You got it, man? A promise! I'll run you out of medicine so all you'll ever have is a slaughterhouse abortion mill in some Mexican border town, *after* you get out of prison."

Elmore shoved Wagnon away with such violence the young man fell down. As Wagnon scrambled sideways to gain his feet, Elmore said, "You were assigned specifically to keep watch on Colonel Brown, to regularly monitor his respiration, temperature, heart action . . . but I come in here and find the colonel literally, *actually*, climbing the wall with pain."

Sullenly, Wagnon said, "I was busy with other—"

"Busy! Doing what, jacking off?"

"I have other duties, and besides that, if he were actually in such pain, he could have called out, or rung the buzzer."

"The more you talk, the more bites you take of your own stupid foot. You know as well as I do, Colonel Brown is the kind of man who would die before he'd let pain make him scream, and don't think, for a single instant, that I overlooked the fact that the Colonel would need an arm five feet long to reach the buzzer. If you want him dead, why don't you simply give him a massive jolt of morphine?"

Shaking with fury, Wagnon said, "I don't have to take that kind of accusation, Major Elmore. I warn you now, I intend to resort to higher authority."

"You mean you're going to suckup Bert Wright and see if you can get a transfer, in plain English. I'll save you the trouble. You are fired. You are hereby, as of this moment, relieved of your command for gross negligence. We kept you, you dumbutt, to try to help you become a man, but you've proved to be a hopeless case. Do you understand me? You are relieved of duty. You will report instantly to your quarters where you will prepare yourself and your personal gear for removal to the army officers' pool in Saigon on first available ground transportation. *Ground* transportation. You're not fit to associate with airmen! Dismissed!" It was all Elmore could do to keep from knocking Wagnon down. Instead he turned back to Brown and heard the door of the recovery room close as Wagnon departed, in haste.

To Elmore's surprise, Brown's eyes batted open, and Brown said, "Nice work, Doc."

"You couldn't have said it better yourself."

Brown felt his face stretch with a grin. "That sure is fine stuff you hit me with; it drove that son of a bitch on his steamroller clear out of sight." Brown did not try to explain the hallucination he'd had; he could tell that Elmore knew Brown referred to something about the pain.

Brown said, "Am I permitted visitors?"

"Let Walker sleep, Joe, OK?"

"When he wakes?"

"I'll send him to you in an hour, but he can stay for only a short time."

"Thirty minutes?"

"Make it twenty."

"How are things going?"

"Not well."

"Have they sent in my replacement?"

"Not yet."

"Who do they have in mind?"

"It's more a matter of who's available."

Brown laughed, thinking of March; the bastard must be sitting up there with his asshole biting holes out of his chair, he was so damned scared Paulson would send him down to take over while Brown recuperated. "What kind of status report did you send out regarding me?"

"Vague," Elmore said. "I thought that's how you'd want it, until you made up your mind."

"Doc, just tell me this: can I make it? Am I going to be all right?"

"If you take care of yourself."

"You know what this job requires of a man. Based upon that, can I do it?"

"I wish it were not a sin to lie. . . . Yes, Colonel, you can make it, if you follow my instructions. The main thing is rest. If you over-extend too early, then the only thing you can expect is pneumonia and the strain could very well have serious effects on your heart. You cannot fly."

"I wouldn't expect that, nor want to, with other men's lives depending upon my physical capabilities. That's asking too much when the situation demands no risk."

"This is enough for now. Rest, try to sleep. I'll send Walker in when he wakes."

Elmore left, and a moment after the door closed, Brown heard voices in the hallway; then the door opened again and Elmore returned with a captain who wore the crossed flint-lock pistols badge on one collar, indicating he was in MPs.

He saluted and said, "Sir, we believe we have the man who fragged you."

"Yes?"

"His name is Stavros, your adjutant's clerk, sir."

"That's ridiculous."

The captain's face went red with embarrassed anger, but he plunged ahead, doggedly. "Sir, we have had the man under surveillance for some time, as a suspected homosexual. He was apprehended in the vicinity of your quarters almost immediately after the attempt upon your life."

"Was he hiding, running away, what?"

The captain's brow wrinkled. "Well, no sir, he wasn't." The captain's mouth moved as though he suddenly tasted something rotten. "As a matter of fact, he had a tray of food and pot of coffee, which he claimed he was taking to your quarters." The captain then rolled his shoulders like a boxer warming up. "But don't worry, sir, we'll get the truth out of him soon enough. We've got him in interrogation now, and these god damn queers—they can't take no heat."

Brown raised his left hand and crooked his forefinger. The captain came across the room and, probably, he had figured something was about to work out quite differently from what he'd planned, when he came in to see the colonel and make a few points with the old man, reporting the news that the fragger was in custody.

Brown looked up at the man, and read the nameplate on the captain's khaki shirt: C, E, PERI. Brown looked up into Peri's eyes. "Captain, release Stavros at once. You, personally, bring him here to me. If he has been touched, other than by use of normal restraint customary in placing a man under arrest, you and every man involved will leave this base in handcuffs and leg-irons under arrest for transportation to the military prison, Vietnam. Stavros was indeed bringing me food, at my orders as issued to him by Captain Walker. Moreover, Stavros is not a homosexual, so your goons can beat on him all day and he won't confess to something he's not. Now get the hell out of my sight!"

The captain's face had gone sickly white and his fat jaws sagged as he listened to Brown. When he turned and left the room, he had the posture and movement of a man stricken with excruciating arthritis.

Elmore repeated his instructions to get some rest and try to sleep. To Brown's surprise, he did fall into a drowse, almost at once.

10

Joe Brown had just awakened when Walker came and saluted, clumsily, with his right hand in a plaster cast. "What the hell now, brown cow?" Joe asked, but he thought that probably he already knew. It took a few minutes, but Brown got the story, and his thought had been correct:

The night before, Walker had gotten into an argument with Paulk in the officers' lounge, and when Paulk pushed it too hard, what a slave-driving bastard Colonel Brown was, Walker had said, "At least he's not a god damn coward, who gets *lost* on night missions."

Paulk was stupid enough, self-conscious enough, and, possibly, drunk enough, so he took a punch at Walker, trying for the Sunday on the blind side as Walker turned away; but a warning shout from Warrant Bass made Walker duck under the punch. He turned and drove a right uppercut into the point of Paulk's jaw, unhinging it on the right side, and breaking it in two places. But Walker discovered, to his dismay, that he, too, had bad hands for fistfighting; and his right was broken in two places, the small bones behind his middle and ringfinger knuckles. Neither man had filed, nor intended to file any charges. A fight in the officers' club is one of the very, very few forms of misconduct an officer can get by with; but even though it never goes into the officer's file, the unbecoming conduct, somehow, always seems to get remembered when the officer next appears before a promotion board and one of the interviewers always asks about it. Always.

To Walker, it did not matter; when his time was up, he was as gone as yesterday's story of the hour on TV news. For Paulk, if what Brown had heard about the pilot was true, it mattered a very great deal. Paulk was an army brat, a lifer, who was doing a tour of duty in Hog gunships because it was expected of him; then he would go back to flying fixed-wing airplanes, a sort of taxi service, Cessna 310s and Twin Bonanzas. It would depend upon how many of Paulk's father's friends sat on the board. It would probably be arranged. Walker was a civilian, would be, by the time Paulk's number came up, so Brown was sure everything would be arranged by then, which Brown thought was a god damn shame; army aviation needed men like Jack Paulk about as much as Joe Brown needed another rectum, right between his eyes.

"How's it going?" asked Brown.

"To hell on greased skids."

"That bad, huh?"

"Worse."

"Tell me."

"The pilots won't fly."

"You mean outright refusals?"

"No, but S-O-S—the same old stuff. They line up for sick call twice a day, they turn the ships back to Marston. They lie in bed with lower back pains of undetermined origin. The whole big blivit, doubled."

"Christ, how long have I been out of it?"

"Three days."

Brown made an effort to get up, but he knew it was useless; his body simply was not buckled back together again.

There was no point in Brown discussing endlessly with Walker the details of how 504 had fallen apart. The fact that the unit was not flying missions was all either needed to know, and were almost powerless to remedy. With his broken hand, Walker could not safely fly a helicopter; Brown couldn't even get out of bed.

Doc Elmore opened the door and held it. Stavros entered, accompanied by two shined and buffed and superbly polished MPs. They were both corporals, and looked like linebacker candidates for any team in the NFL. They grooved salutes, and the one on the right side and just behind Stavros said, "Prisoner delivered as ordered, sir."

"How can the man be called prisoner when I ordered him released?"

The MPs looked at one another, at the colonel, at Doc Elmore, at Stavros as though it were all his fault, then the same one mumbled, "Well, sir, Colonel, I mean, ah, that's what we always say when we take a pris— a person, some soljer somewheres and turn him over to someone else, Colonel, sir."

Brown asked Stavros, "Did they hit you?"

Stavros shook his head. He seemed to be trying to look back over both shoulders at the same time, at the MPs, like a spooky bronc watching the man astride his back.

"Can't you talk?"

"My . . . throat's . . . kind of—" He blinked and tears ran from his dark eyes. Brown motioned and Elmore took Stavros' arm and led him to a chair. He took the medical flashlight from his smock pocket, opened the clerk's mouth and shined the light inside. He gently palpatated Stavros' throat, and the kid flinched away, grunting in pain. Brown shot a fast look at the MPs. Both stood at rigid parade rest looking straight ahead, unblinking; they might have been made of stone. Brown turned his eyes on Elmore.

"The larynx is partially crushed, from some kind of outside pressure. As a guess, I'd say he got hacked across the throat, with the edge of a hand perhaps, possibly something else. The damage inside is—" Elmore lifted his shoulders. "It looks as though something about the size of a five-cell flashlight, the barrel portion, has been repeatedly rammed down his throat." Then Doc Elmore's eyebrows shot up, and he examined the clerk's throat again, nodded and stepped back, said, "Drop your trousers and drawers."

Dumbly, tears running down his face, Stavros complied. Joe Brown had been raised in ranching country; he knew what the marks looked like, when an electric cattle prod has been applied to bare flesh. Brown looked up at the

MPs, and he felt under his left side, covered by the sheet, and found the .45 Colt pistol. Without taking his gaze from the military policeman, Brown asked Stavros, "Were these men your interrogators?"

Elmore said, "He's holding up just one finger."

Brown pulled the .45 from under the sheet covering his body and laid it on his lap. "Which one of them?"

Elmore said, "He's pointing toward the one on the left." But Brown already knew because the big man's face had gone the color of his white gloves, and Brown had, too long, been an athlete not to know, to see, when a man was about to make a move. He picked up the .45 and pointed it at the man's face. He told the other MP, "Disarm him."

The other MP looked stupidly around the room, as though he'd awakened on an alien planet. Brown ordered him again, voice cold, hard, flat, carrying; and the MP seemed to jump outside his skin, crawl back inside, and hastily begin performing his habitual routine. "OK, buddy, hands over your head, turn and face the wall—"

"You dumbutt," Brown shouted, "just take his god damn pistol from him and put the handcuffs on him."

The MP made the skin jump again, out and back inside, and did as ordered. When the MP under arrest was handcuffed, Brown asked Stavros, "Was he the only one?"

Stavros shook his head, pointed at the MP, then held up two fingers. Brown said, "He and one other?" Stavros shook his head and held up three fingers, and pointed at the MP. He managed one word, "Viets."

"This man and two Viet cops, is that correct?"

Stavros nodded agreement.

Brown told Walker, "Find them, bring them here."

Walker said, "Right, Skipper." He motioned to the MP guarding the other, "Let's go," and they all went out as Brown told Stavros, "As soon as the doctor permits you, type up a complete statement of exactly what happened, from the moment you were arrested until you saw that MP taken into custody."

Stavros nodded, wiping tears from his eyes, and went

out with Doc Elmore as Walker came back into the room. Joe Brown said, "So soon?"

"No, sir. I detailed Bass to that job. Something's come up I thought you'd better hear about at once. We've located Edwards."

"Where did he go down?"

Words lathered with contempt, Walker said, "He didn't go down. He just peeled off and landed at the god damn slickship base, then went up the side of the ship and peeled back the cowling and spent half the night *working* on his engine." Walker jerked his chin toward the maintenance hangar. "Marston says he's sure, certain in his own mind, that Edwards sabotaged the engine after he landed. But—"

"Impossible to prove in a courtmartial."

"Exactly. First place, no witnesses. Edwards wouldn't allow anyone up there to help him, not even hold a flashlight. Marston just returned and told me this. He repaired the damage and flew the ship in. Edwards and his crew are in debriefing interrogation."

"That should make good reading. He's had three days to get the story just like he wants it."

"Three thousand words of the very best."

"How's the chow been?"

"Still great. You put the fear of the stinging tail into that tub of guts over there, Morris."

"Fear of the stinging tail?"

"Scorpion," Walker said, grinning, "That's what the men are calling you now. That you always got your butt over your shoulders about something around here, and it stings like hell when you do something to make it right."

"Just pass the word that I come from Durango, too," Brown said, smiling. "Down there they raise scorpions the size of a cigarette pack and its sting can kill a horse."

Walker shook his head, grinning; then he sobered and asked, "You still want to see Hopler?"

"How is he?"

"In a hell of a bad way, Colonel. Doc Elmore tried to go along a bit, and bring Hopler down easy; but Hop got

96

Latest U.S. Government
tests of all cigarettes
show True is
lower in both
tar and nicotine
than 98% of all other
cigarettes sold.

Think about it.
Shouldn't your next cigarette be True?

Regular: 12 mg. ''tar'', 0.7 mg. nicotine,
Menthol: 12 mg. ''tar'', 0.8 mg. nicotine, av. per cigarette, FTC Report Feb. '73.

Latest U.S. Government
tests of all menthol
cigarettes show
True is lower
in both tar and
nicotine than 98% of
all other menthols sold.

Think about it.
Shouldn't your next cigarette be True?

mean, then tried to break out, and tried bribing some of the medics; so Elmore threw him in the padded room to come down cold turkey."

"I'll back him on it, all the way; but if the press gets hold of that item, you know what it means."

Walker nodded sourly.

"What about the Spitter, what the hell's his name?" The guy whose jaw I cracked?"

"He's OK, all wired up, a block of wood screwed to his face and he's on baby food now instead of straight liquid diet." Laughing, Walker said, "His real name is Travis Charles, sergeant door-gunner."

"Assign him to my ship." Brown thought for a moment, "And who was that other sergeant thought he was such a badass, Hopler's buddy?"

"Bynum."

"OK, assign him to me, also. Has he got the word through his skull yet?"

"He's no subject for an aftershave or deodorant commercial, but it's no longer like lying down in a hog pen when you stand next to him."

"What else?"

"All the enlisted men are whining the blues because their club's still closed."

"Pass the word, the EM club stays closed until we find out who fragged old Scorpion Brown."

Walker cocked his head and looked curiously at Brown. He licked his lips and shook his head. "Sir, I—Well, I assumed—I thought you *knew*!"

"Knew *what*? Come on, Walker!"

"They've got him. Despite what that blubber-butted Perl looks like, and his slowmotion thinking, he knows his job. When he left here to have Stavros released, he discovered that his men had picked up another man last night, trying to get out through the wire. They were just holding him for trying to AWOL, figuring they had the fragger when they nailed Stavros."

"How can they be sure? I mean look what they did to that kid, with that god damn cattle prod on his genitals

97

and ramming it down his throat. What did those lousy Viet cops, and maybe some of our people, too—what did they do with this other kid, put a bicycle lock around his balls and tighten it a notch at a time till he'd have told them he was Ho Chin Minh?"

"Not at all. He just copped. Well, not exactly. He made a speech, human dignity, civil rights, tyranny, and you are not only a Scorpion, you are *quote* the absolute personification of a WASP racist, a sadistic latent homosexual, as are most army lifers, particularly Academy-trained officers, and—well, I guess I've forgotten just how he put the rest of it, *end quote*. Oh, yes, he also called upon all blacks now enslaved by the military forces in Vietnam to lay down their arms. And contribute to the Angela Davis Defense Fund.

"The shrinks have him now, and he'll probably beat it."

All Brown could do was shake his head, and then he finally thought to ask, "Who is he?"

"Think about it a moment, and I won't even have to give you one guess."

"Either the kid fondling the grenade that first day, or the one with the MAT 50."

"Right on, as the saying goes, the first time. The other kid was white; he just hadn't washed recently."

Elmore came in and said flatly, "That's enough," and Walker left without a word while Elmore popped Joe Brown's sore bottom with yet another injection.

11

Doc Elmore stood with his long arms folded and gave every appearance of a man totally deaf, then abruptly raised his hand, palm toward Colonel Joseph Paul Brown.

"No, say again, no. You cannot fly."

"God damn it, I can *walk*, I can read your charts. Any man who can walk can fly. It's a sitting-down sort of job."

"No."

"Aw, now—"

"None of the honey after all that vinegar, if you please, Colonel."

"All right, then— When?"

"The day after tomorrow."

"Tomorrow?"

"Possibly, but *only* after we run those checks once more, thoroughly." Elmore uncrossed his arms and came across the room. "Joe, we had to pump a lot of stuff into you, antibiotics and plain old dope for the pain. It just isn't safe yet. Some of that junk is persistent, stays in the system for days. Christ, you know the rules. You're not supposed to fly for twelve hours after taking a simple little antihistamine dosage. Why the hell ride me?"

"OK, so what about Walker?"

"Don't be silly."

"He says he could probably make it with a good tight wrapping of elastic bandaging."

"Not yet. I'll X-ray again in a few days, and then perhaps we can take off the cast and use Ace bandaging. No promises."

"Meanwhile, the whole unit sits on its ass on the ground, claiming lower back pains and sinusitis and ulcer symptoms—"

"And I don't ground a one of them unless I'm convinced, and I convince about as easy as a flat-broke hundred-dollar hooker that she ought to lay a little freebie on some John. I can't *make* them fly, but I can make damned sure they don't use this office to keep out of the air."

So that's how it went, the next two days. Joe Brown prowling the area like a caged jaguar, laying that scorpion sting on everything in sight, and catching up on the increasingly endless paperwork. He had found, through WO Bass' efforts, the two Viet cops who had tortured Stavros with the cattle prod, and they were now in jail themselves . . . or rather, Joe Brown supposed they were. Their remaining jailed depended entirely upon how much money they had accumulated through years of graft and corruption and the friends in power they'd made. How Stavros got the burns and abrasions inside his throat was solved: the American MP had told his Viet pals Stavros was a fruiter, so they thought they'd see how funny the clerk looked sucking off something that bit back; they rammed the mean end of the cattle prod down Stavros' throat and thumbed the button, and when he pleaded with them, one of the Viet cops gave him a karate chop across the throat to stop the screaming. Brown hoped the sons of bitches liked it out there in their new quarters, the tiger cages on Long Binh Island. The American MP had copped out completely on the whole bit to gain the immunity from prosecution offer, so he walked free and easy around the base, but had no one much to talk to. Even the utter nastiness of this filthy little war had not brutalized the ordinary base-camp soldiers to the point where they condoned such behavior by their own. It wasn't as if they were frontline infantrymen who'd seen what the VC and the NVA regulars were capable of doing, and regularly did to U.S. troops when captured, such as skinning alive, staking down over ant beds, emasculation and disemboweling.

Hopler was out now on PAL, prisoner at large, status. Being a warrant officer, that meant he was free to come

100

and go without MP escort to meals and for calls of nature, and the rest of the time was confined to his quarters in the BOQ. He looked like a cold ambulatory corpse, eyes like two holes burned in a dirty saddle-blanket, moved as though strung together with rusty wire.

Paulk had made behind-the-scene connections, probably through his father, and was transferred out to the big hospital in Saigon, and no one expected his return. Brown was particularly glad Paulk had found a way to get out, off the base, because he was malignant, cancerous—his behavior had, perhaps, if not probably, given other pilots who did not want to fly a way out. Fly the mission so they couldn't be accused of outright refusal, but then get "lost."

Brown simply could not figure a way to handle the case of Edwards. Purely and simply the man had peeled off out of the fire fight, claiming engine trouble, landed and then deliberately sabotaged his own gunship; but it was equally purely and simply impossible to prove. At one point, Brown actually found himself thinking how once he was, personally, able to fly again, he would assign Edwards the lead, then shoot him down. The actual thought sickened Brown, because murder was not his business, and besides that, what about the undeserving crewmen who would die with Edwards, and the destruction of a million-dollars-plus worth of aircraft? . . . What he finally settled upon was ordering a formal inquiry, a sort of military meeting resembling a grand jury to investigate the case. No matter what the outcome, after Edwards' crewmen and other witnesses at the scene, and Marston's expert testimony, Edwards would be smeared with so much shit he'd be through as an army flying officer. That's all Brown cared about, getting rid of him and the kind of infectious "rather be a live coward" attitude that had somehow infested 504.

That was Brown's motive in letting Hopler be seen around the base. The poor scarecrow-looking pitiful man might serve as an example, perhaps frighten just one other man, to have absolutely nothing more to do with hard

drugs. Find the rottenness, exorcise it, exhibit it, let the men have a whiff of the putrefaction, and after they finished puking, maybe it would drive the blood to their god damn skulls and wise them up. Brown wanted his men with a lot on their minds, every time they saw something like Hopler, and Stavros, and the Downhill Gang brand painted on the Hog gunships: $\overline{\text{OO}}$
$$\overline{\text{MM}}$$

When old Spitter, Sergeant doorgunner Travis Charles, was released from the hospital, Brown called him in. "You've been assigned to my ship."

"Yes, sir."

Brown noticed the sergeant's tone was absolutely neutral. He asked, "No complaints, no request for transfer?"

"I'm in the army, sir; and do what I'm told."

"I can remember when you didn't have quite that attitude."

"I remember, too, when I had no respect for any officer I knew, except Mr. Walker."

"You'll fly with me?"

"I will, sir," and there was just a hint of tone of expectation if not eagerness in Charles' voice.

"I will ask you the same question that I put to Captain Walker. Are you putting the con-job on me? Are you sweet-talking me to my face while you run the ridges behind my back getting statements so you can file charges against me for busting your ass?"

Sergeant Charles laughed. "I wouldn't have a chance. I *did* swing on you first." He laughed again. "Since lying in the hospital, I've figured I came out of it lucky as hell. You could have shot me with that god damn—excuse me, sir—you would have gotten by with shooting me. And I've talked to Captain Walker, too, Colonel. If I can't ride a ship with you, then I want to work for him."

"If you'd rather ride with Walker. . . ." Brown let it hang there.

"I'm already assigned to your crew, sir. I'd like to stay on."

"Why?"

"Because when one day my son asks me what did you do in the war, daddy, I want to tell him I flew gunship missions in a Hucy Hog. I don't want to tell him I laid around jacking myself off at a gunship base where we had no pilots who'd go in there."

Brown got up and they shook hands and he told Charles to find Bynum and send him to the office. The short man was no longer tubby, no longer wore a perpetual twist on his thin lips; and he was clean. Brown said, "You got the word on your assignment?"

"Yes, sir."

"And you don't like it."

"If I may be permitted to speak frankly with the Colonel, sir."

"I don't care for the third-person address, Bynum. I'm standing right here in front of you, so look at me and talk to me, like a man, if you know how."

"I'd like a transfer, sir."

"Any particular place?"

Bynum was so surprised he could not speak for a moment. Then he drew a deep breath and said, "Any place out of 504."

"Excellent. Have Stavros type up immediate transfer orders. You won't have far to go. Just across the base to the other gunship outfit, which has—in case you don't know— the highest record of missions accomplished of any Hog unit during the war. And in case you've forgotten, this war's been going on almost ten years now. You many not want to fly with me, buddy-boy, but you will fly, you will fly every day, all day long, until your tour of duty ends or they award you the Royal Order of the Mattress Cover and ship your remains back home to momma. Dismissed."

"But sir, you didn't give me a chance—"

"Wrong, buddy-boy, you've had chances till they ran out your ears. And you can't act like a man. Your mouth's all mealy. I'd have thought more of you, and forgiven you, if you'd come in and called me a hardassed old prick, instead of giving me the third-person bit and weasling

103

around. You asked for a transfer and you got it, so take it and if you make it out alive you can go back home to selling shit for a living, or whatever kind of work something like you does. Dismissed."

Brown finished out the day with paperwork, and after he'd showered, shaved, changed into clean khaki, he went to the officers' club. He edged up to the bar, and noticed how the men moved away from him; and expected them to do so. Then, Walker got up from an old overstuffed chair and walked all the way across the room to stand beside his commander and tell the enlisted bartender, "Give the Colonel what he wants and put it on my tab." A moment later Bass edged in, not quite so closely, but close enough so the others saw where his sympathies lay, and he too set one up for the three of them. Brown got his Old Parr and bottled water, sipped, lit a cigar despite Doc Elmore's orders, then turned and faced the room, looking at the men. He looked at them one by one, starting on the left, and stared them down, one by one, until he'd sneered at the last of them, over on the right. Brown became aware of the wall to his left. On it was the brand, and the name:

504th Helicopter Unit

$$\frac{O\ O}{MM}$$

The Downhill Gang

Brown smiled widely and raised his glass toward the wall, then drained his glass. He turned back to the bar and as Bass moved in a bit closer, Brown said, "Set us up three more." As the bartender worked, Brown asked, "Who's idea was that?"

Walker said, "Sergeant Charles put one up in the EM club." Walker grinned and said, "I think he lied a little, and told the NCOIC it was your order. I liked it so much I asked him to fix us up with the same."

Brown nodded and puffed his cigar, without inhaling,

104

as Doc Elmore came up to stand beside them. "Following the doctor's orders precisely, I see."

"Hey, Doc, you never said I couldn't drink, and I'm not inhaling."

Elmore grinned. "You two come by and see me after lunch tomorrow, and I'll see what I can do; but I must be bribed. Barman! A C.C. and gingerale, if you please."

"Lord, what a waste of good Canadian whisky, putting that sweet glop in it," Walker said, wrinkling his nose.

"Making the world go around, sonny; that's all. Different strokes for different folks."

Walker paid for the drink as the four of them laughed aloud again.

Apparently a large-boned warrant officer with a red goatee sitting near the old jukebox did not like the camaraderie and fellowship he saw at the bar, so he fed in coins, pulled the box away from the wall, and turned it up as loud as it would go. Brown figured the man was either drunk, or accidentally punched the wrong buttons, or was making some rather stupid effort at sarcasm, for the room suddenly filled with sound that made the walls bulge—guitars, Nashville Sound, and Merle Haggard:

"We don't smoke marijuana in Muskogee,
We don't take our trips on L S D . . . ."

The four men at the bar all looked at one another, laughed hilariously, finished their drinks, then strode out in pairs, Brown and Elmore leading, Walker and Bass coming along behind.

Brown reported to Elmore at 1300 hours the following afternoon, after a light lunch, and passed his flight medical check. Walker was also there, but after an X-ray, Elmore ignored Walker's vehement protests and put the hand back in plaster.

Brown went down on the line to look over the ships. Of course they were in the finest possible shape that Marston and his crew could put them, which was not hard since the ships had not been flying. As he walked around them, Brown saw that in some cases the Downhill Gang had been blotted out by spray paint, and juvenile phrases such as Fuck Brown and Brown Eats It had been crudely sprayed on. Brown took out his notebook and wrote on a page and handed it to Marston. "Cut a stencil and have these two phrases put on every ship, and use Day-Glo orange paint."

Marston looked at the page and laughed aloud, then shook his head. "The one I dig, but what's the other?"

"That's *con safos*. It's a Mexican border slang term. It can't be translated precisely, but what it means is that anything you say about me or my gang simply bounces off us and rebounds to stick on you, doubled and with handles."

"Ah, I get it. Where it says, well, you know—Eff Brown, by saying *con safos* you're replying screw you twice."

"Plus your sisters and mother."

Marston laughed, shaking his head. Brown said, "The other, I want big, in large letters, so get hold of Sergeant Charles, unless you have someone who can letter free-hand in the shop."

"Yes, sir, I have a man."

"I want it done now."

The work drew a crowd. The Mexican-Americans in the unit spent all afternoon trying to explain to the other men in the unit what *con safos* meant, and many of them looked very bitter that Colonel Scorpion Brown should multiple-cross them in such fashion and thus leave them defenseless. Because nobody has yet invented a *con safos con safos,* which Brown actually had painted on most of the gunships in the way it usually appears on walls, car doors, sides of buildings . . . C/S. Instead of spelling it out.

But it was the other that really attracted the most attention that late afternoon as the men of 504 went to chow. In brilliant fluorescent orange lettering along the side of each Hog gunship read:

Brown claimed no originality for this bit. Among the first purchases he'd made in the Saigon flea market on his first tour of duty in Vietnam was a red-white-blue banner six feet long and ten inches wide with the same expression stenciled on it with black ink. It was now on the wall of his "camp" back in Arizona. . . .

Brown went to the officers' mess and found Bass and sat down beside him while the young warrant ate his supper. "Will you fly door gunner for me?"

Bass dropped his fork, spluttered, started to say something about being a pilot, and then said, "Hell, yes!"

Brown thanked him, drank a cup of hot tea and ate some toast. He was on his way back to his office when Walker came up to him, fast and white-faced.

"There's a Special Forces outfit at Bn Ca that's in desperate trouble. Orders from Saigon, everything that can fly and carry ordnance is ordered to scramble!"

"OK, alert the duty officer and tell him to ring the chime, and all we can do . . ." Brown seemed to choke on the words, ". . . is see what happens." He ran toward his office and climbed into flying gear while the klaxon began to *ooo-gah* through the evening sky.

Brown stood on the platform and gave a hurried briefing, locating Bn Ca on the wall chart, informing the pilots of the situation. Then he stood aside and let Walker give the navigation information, the map coordinates, the course to fly and the nearest alternate airports in case anyone had to put down a crippled ship. Brown stood on the platform and looked at the men and he almost wanted to cry. Some of them were not even going through the motions of copying down the information. He took over again when Walker finished and all he could think to say was, "This isn't like the last one. This isn't to get out a bunch of Viets who got themselves into trouble. These are *our* guys, a United States Army Special Forces Unit." Then he stepped off the platform and went out the door.

The men followed him out the door of the briefing shack, and approximately half of them headed directly for Doc Elmore's office. Those who did not went to their ships, puttered around, preflighted with the exaggerated care of an astronaut looking over his lunar landing module before departing the moon. Sergeant Charles was ready and he showed Bass how he'd learned a trick or two that increased reloading speed. Brown cranked up and warmed and when he was ready, he radioed the others. "Downhill Gang, Downhill Gang, this is Downhill Leader, prepare to lift off. . . . *Lift*off and follow me!" Only three other ships became airborne. The first of those made a skimming high circle and returned to land. The other two followed for about a mile, then one of them returned to base, radioing he'd had a partial failure of his electrical system. The third flew up alongside Brown and with hand signals indicated he had no radio, then turned back.

Brown flew on alone, tears rimming the lower lids of his green eyes as he tuned in his radio to the frequency of the air controller over the battered Bn Ca SF base. When Brown arrived over the embattled camp, it was like looking down into the bottom of hell; not even Dante or Hemingway or any of the best hell-describers, had ever given any reader a view of what it looked like down there.

The base was typically constructed, somewhat like an old frontier-post during the Indian wars in the American Southwest. It was made of upright thick posts, braced and concreted into place, barbed wire double and triple aprons stretching out all around the triangular-shaped fort. It was strung with boobytraps, claymore mines and other explosive charges; and the VC had penetrated those outer defenses, at the cost of how many men only God knew, if he was watching.

Alone, all Brown could do was join up with another unit, put himself under the mission leader's command and make his runs, expend his ordnance, manage to get both Bass and Charles slightly wounded, take ground fire that knocked his ship full of holes but did no significant damage; and then, return to base. He had radioed ahead, for

Doc Elmore met him on the ramp, tended to the wounded, ordered Bass to hospital, and Bass appealed to Brown, and all Brown could say was, "Doc, I've got to have two gunners."

Elmore nodded, gave Bass some pills. "If the pain in that place above the knee gets to crawling up inside your groin, take these. They will affect your depth-perception some, probably, since it's nighttime, but the pain will put you down if you let it get too bad."

The armorers worked fast and airframe mechs had patching almost in place when Brown decided, aloud, "Why the hell fly this wreck when we've got ready ships all over the place."

He led Bass and Charles to the next Hog down the line, that had turned back because of claimed radio failure. Brown tried the radio and it worked perfectly. He cranked up and warmed and lifted off. As he banked away, he looked down and saw Walker throwing his hat on the concrete, pointing his finger, raging at the men who'd come to stand and watch.

The second mission was a repeat of the first, except that Brown saw the Special Forces men were losing. He joined up with another command, made his runs, got off his rockets, emptied his machine guns, and banked away to shove for base when some lucky son-of-a-bitching Charley with an AK-47 anti-aircraft rifle almost shot the Hog from under Brown. He fought it and kept it flying: skill, guts, absolute knowledge of the limitations of the airplane and himself, and he got the Hog back to base. And found that he could not land. The engine would run only at full rpm. The instant Brown began to reduce power, the bastard tried to quit him. He made a pass circling around the base and figured out what to do. He called the crew and told them to strap themselves and prepare for crash landing. Charles replied, "All set, sir."

Brown said, "Bass?"

"He's dead, Colonel."

"OK, son, here we go."

109

Brown went far out, kept the power on because that was the only way the ship would run, flew lower and lower until his undercarriage skimmed and even touched briefly a time or two, and then Brown shut everything off. The engine quit instantly; the ship tilted crazily, righted, hit on its undercarriage, slid, skittered sideways, tilted up as though to go over on its back, fell back to earth and made two swooping full circles as it, finally, came to a stop, afire.

Stunned, but conscious, Brown unbuckled and crawled back out, feeling Charles' hands helping him. There were flames everywhere. Brown hit the ground and grabbed the sergeant's arm. Charles shouted, "Mr. Bass!"

"NO! She's going to blow any moment! *Run!*"

The blast of the explosion knocked them both down. They rose and ran again, and Brown saw how erractically Charles moved, and shouted, "You hit?" Charles only shook his head and kept going as the fire trucks passed them and an ambulance screeched to a halt beside them. Charles immediately sat down and took his sheath knife and cut the thong lacings of his right boot and jerked it off, sighing, "Jesus!"

A piece of metal off the exploding Hog had pierced the heel of his boot, just enough so that a needlelike point embedded itself into his heel. Looking at it, Brown saw it was hardly more than a deep scratch, but he knew it must have been some kind of hell, running with that sliver of metal gouging Charles' heel every step.

Brown knelt beside the sergeant. "How about it?"

"Shit, I'm ready! Soon's I get this boot fixed." From the crowd gathered around, a mechanic stepped forward and took Charles' boot, and with a pair of pliers worked the metal splinter from the bootheel. He offered it to Charels, grinning, "Make a good souvenir."

"Frig souvenirs. All I ever want out of this cruddy god damn war is my own ass, all in one piece." He looked around, "Which one of you heroes got a bootlace you'd loan out overnight?"

110

Brown asked Elmore, "Will you OK Walker for door-gunner duty?"

"Joe, you're not going out again."

"Doc, would you tell me that if the commander of that Special Forces unit were standing here?"

Stavros stepped forward, and in his voice that would remain husky all the rest of his life, he said, "Sir, I'm checked out as door-gunner."

Brown said, "Let's go, son," and brutally shoved his way through the crowd who'd gathered to gawk, deliberately cracking his elbow across WO Woodley's nose, stamping down hard on 2/Lt. Mooney's foot. As Walker caught up to him, Brown said, "I forgot to tell you, ship that Woodley. We may not be able to make these bastards fly, but at least let's get rid of the fucking culls while we're trying to get something going. And what about that big turd in the club the other night, the one turned on the juke?"

"Webb, commissioned warrant."

"Is he a cull?"

"I say no. He's a mustang, up from the ranks, solid, excellent pilot."

"How the hell does anyone know, since he doesn't fly?"

Walker didn't say anything.

"He usually on the sauce like the other night?"

"Only lately."

"Meaning what?"

"Meaning he's a lot like I was, I think. What he feels more than anything else is shame, that he's allowed himself to get infected with whatever it was hit this outfit and flattened it."

"OK, see what you can do to warm him up, and any others you think—" Brown didn't finish. He reached the side of the helicopter that its pilot claimed had a partial failure of the electrical system. He asked Marston, "This ship redlined?"

"There's nothing wrong with this aircraft."

Brown looked over his shoulder at Charles and Stavros. "Ready?" They both nodded. "My door-gunners are

111

sergeants. Put Stavros' promotion through, effective now." Walker smiled and tossed off a salute. "Will do, instanter!"

Brown got settled into his seat and put the office in business. He had his head down, running through some of his checks, when over the intercom radio he heard Charles say, "Looks like we've got some company this run."

Brown's head jerked up and he looked around. Three other helicopters had blades turning. For a moment, Joe Brown did not know what came over him, when he felt a big up-pushing something rise in his throat and he thought maybe he cried a little.

The third mission was worse than the second, despite the crash landing. When Downhill Gang, four gunships, reached Bn Ca, the Viet Cong had breached the west side of the triangular-shaped fort, and the Special Forces commander had decided to get his men out. But the same problem arose as the last time; the slickship-evacuation-helicopter unit on call to carry troops was the same bunch of yellowbacked South Vietnamese pilots as on the earlier mission.

Brown called the air controller. "I'll take my four Hogs in and bring out as many as I can."

For a moment there was no answer; then in a tired, virtually sobbing voice, the AC said, "Thank you, Colonel."

All it was, and not in some comparative sense, but actually, was a trip down into the depths of hell on a helicopter. Joe Brown remembered he'd read a book one time about some Marines in Korea; and some young kid said all he ever wanted if granted a single wish was, "Give Me Tomorrow." And later on in the book, the writer had one of the guys die while in an evacuation chopper, a sort of illusion or something, about a combat man going to heaven by helicopter.

That was the other end of that ride.

Brown swept in, pulled up and hovered high directly over the center of the fort. Then he lowered by autorota-

112

tion, letting the ship swing around and around, slowly, as he came down, so he kept up a continuous stream of fire from his rockets and fixed machine guns and the door-gunners had fresh targets continuously. Brown put it down; a group of men charged from a concrete blockhouse and dived into the side hatches of the Hog and Brown got out lifting off in an almost vertical bank to the right. The ship had a heavy, soggy feel to it and he knew he was over gross weight, so he fired off his remaining rockets and expended some machinegun ammo and intercomed to Charles, "Tell those boys to move as far forward as possible to help trim; we're riding with an assheavy center of gravity."

Brown felt the difference in the handling of the ship almost at once as the passengers crowded forward. He loitered overhead, watching his other ships go in, and like miracles, slaying dragons or driving the stake through a vampire's heart, they all got out. It looked as though they rose straight up through an impossible crisscross of small arms fire, tracers, AK-47 cannon, handgrenades, and there was some enraged VC down there shooting his fucking little Russian automatic pistol at them. . . .

(You get the high ones and I'll get the low
ones, says the man with the club in his hand
standing beside the pistoleer)

The Special Forces commander was on the last ship out, and after he shook Walker's hand, he came across the ramp and stopped before Brown. For a moment, the two men simply looked at one another, then tears began to track down the jungle-suited colonel's face. Joe Brown said, "How are you, Bob?"

Colonel Laya said, choking, "You redskin bastard— You crazy Indian son of a bitch—Thanks." He grabbed Joe Brown's hand and jerked him forward and pounded Brown on the back, and then together they went to see what it cost.

Plenty.

Stavros was dead, shot through the head. The doorgunner that had flown the very first mission with Brown,

Pat Beach, who'd been in Walker's ship, could not be found; presumably he'd been shot and fallen out of the Hog at Bn Ca. With but five exceptions, all of the SF men were wounded, one man in six places; two of them were dead, having died of wounds during the evacuation. Commissioned Warrant Webb had been shot through both arms, yet somehow managed to fly his Hog back to base and land it safely, then passed out.

Walker's fingers were purple with constricted blood under the elastic bandage. He had taken a sheath knife and cut the cast off his hand, wrapped it with Ace bandaging and flew the mission.

To Brown's utter surprise, and dismay, he learned that his maintenance officer, Marston, had flown the third ship. Brown was so angry at first, and then so proud, he could not speak. Finally he just went over and shook Marston's hand, and the moment he let go, Marston shouted, "All right, what's all this god damn gawking around? Get to work on these aircraft."

Brown went through debriefing interrogation first, then dragged himself to his office, making three tracks. He found a bottle of Old Parr and poured one, had just taken a sip when someone rapped on the door. "Come."

Woodley entered, went through all the military courtesy routine, asked permission to speak with the colonel, and Brown ate his can off about the third-person approach, then asked the man what he wanted.

"Permission to stay in the outfit, sir."

Brown laughed in the man's face, sobered, said, "Permission refused. Get off this base tonight." He took a step toward Woodley and the man backed hastily out the door and Brown never saw him again, except once. . . .

A moment later Brown's telephone rang, and without preamble Doc Elmore said, "Depending entirely upon the extent of tissue damage and possible blood poisoning, I will or will not file formal charges against Captain Dale L. Walker."

"Hey, Doc! I didn't—"

"I am aware of that, Colonel. I'm just telling you that

114

you may wish to begin nosing around for a new adjutant. I will not have my orders defied."

"Hey, Doc, there's an old friend of yours over here in my office. How about coming in to say hello?"

Warily, Elmore said, "You know how many casualties we have to care for, but I suppose—what old friend, who?"

"Parr's his name."

"I don't drink the god damn scotch and you know it. Tastes like burnt corks to me. Goodbye!"

Brown got the telephone away from his ear before the crash on the other end. He poured another drink, sipped and unzipped his flight suit. The odor that came wafting up from inside there would, Brown thought, make a buzzard gag. He stripped off, stopping now and then to nip at the amber he poured from the squat bottle, then showered and shaved and lotioned and even squirted some stuff under his arms that was supposed to contain some kind of glop that caused lesions on the lungs, or was it on the brain? On the brain was OK; you had to be crazy to follow this line of work, anyway On the lungs, not so good; it might keep a man from passing his medical. Brown fell down on his bunk, naked, and went to sleep. It was zero-four-thirty-one hours, 0431—thirty-one minutes past four o'clock in the morning.

A few minutes past six, the klaxon sounded and 504 scrambled, getting ten ships into the air. Two turned back, with malfunctions that Marston later verified as legitimate. The mission was into the U Minh area of the delta and cost one ship down, crew rescued, one doorgunner dead in Poole's ship.

They had time for breakfast and then flew another mission, all ships returned, no wounded or dead. As they sat down for lunch, the klaxon went again. It was a bitter, raging, sucked-in mess where a regiment of VC had ambushed a convoy of trucks carrying ARVN Rangers; and when the gunships came in, at least ten AK-47s opened up on them. Two ships went down instantly in flames, pilots shot to pieces, crews crushed and mangled and burned. Two more, including Brown were heavily damaged, but Brown had the satisfaction of flushing one AK-47 gunner from his hiding place. Brown slowed the Hog and let the man run, carrying his big, longbarreled weapon, running hard and fast, head down, across an open area west of the road ambush; then, the man seemed to become aware of the muttering sound so close above and behind him; and he stopped and turned and Brown turned him to jelly with the fixed guns on the Hog.

They got the whole afternoon off.

They were allowed to eat supper in peace.

The clubs were supposed to open at 1800, seven p.m., but Brown had a feeling, so he delayed letting the flyers at the booze. At 1825 hours they scrambled again, six ships, a milk run: an FAC had spotted some fires in a free-fire zone, an area known to be totally controlled and inhabited by VC, so FAC called for a fire mission. The FAC was right. On his second pass, W. O. Poole got a huge secondary explosion—an ammo dump or fuel storage. The 504th got the rest of the night off.

The outfit flew two missions next day, three the day after that. Brown noticed something. Someone in the shops had cut stencils and on the flight suits, the work shirts, the sides of tents, on building walls, even on the tall white caps worn by the cooks and bakers began to appear:

$$\frac{O\ O}{MM}$$

Brown even noticed one man with the brand crudely tatooed on his forearm. The captain in charge of the officers' mess and club had gotten hold of some Viet craftsman, or sent off to Japan, and had all the glasses and mugs inscribed with the brand.

The transformation snowballed. Doc Elmore and his men had no patients and nothing to do. The medics began sneaking rides aboard the gunships on missions. One evening as Brown passed the EM club, he heard a man singing, accompanying himself with guitar. Though the tune, the melody, was familiar to Brown, some country-western song, the words of the song were about Old Scorpion Joe Brown and the Downhill Gang. Brown turned away with tears in his eyes.

The next day, 504 flew three missions, then came orders from Saigon to stand down, for complete IRAN: inspect, replace as necessary; send deserving men on R&R, training of replacement personnel. Brown had personal orders to HQ, Saigon, and that afternoon a Blue Canoe, the army version of the Cessna 310, came for him. He reported in to March, and Colonel March took him directly into General Paulson's office. There was a small gathering of officers there, including a two-star man from U.S. Army, Far East. They didn't make a big deal of it. The two-star man read a few laudatory paragraphs off a hunk of paper, then pinned a Distinguished Service Medal on Joe Brown's shirt and shook his hand.

Joe Brown thought it was all very nice, but he was thirsty and it was hot in the room with all the people, despite the air conditioning; and he started smiling his way toward the door, unfastening the bit of metal and ribbon from his shirt, when General Paulson said, "Joe, just a few minutes more."

They waited in muted silence, small-talking aimlessly, until there was a knock on the door, and at Paulson's command the door opened and Colonel Bob Laya entered. Once more, he brought the real odor of death and gunsmoke right into a quiet place. He looked at Brown and winked. Then said to Paulson and to the two-star man. "Please forgive my tardiness, there was—"

"We know," said the two-star man. "It's perfectly all right, Colonel Laya. But let's get on with it now you're here."

The two-star man took up another box and another piece of paper and handed them to Laya. Laya accepted them and turned to face Joe Brown. "Redskin, this is one of the great high points of my life, and you'd better believe it; because if you had not done what this paper

117

says you did, I would not be allowed the privilege of reading it to you. I'd be dead in a shithole named Bn Ca."

Both Paulson and the two-star man coughed.

Laya grinned, unfolded the paper and read the citation and then pinned on the Distinguished Service Cross. The difference between the two medals was like the difference between a man running a dog out of his yard with a stick, and a lone cop winning a gunfight against five armed gunmen.

A DSM is a hunk of crap like the Legion of Merit that high-ranking officers hand around to one another for outstanding ability in paper shuffling, usually called exceptional management skills. It's like the watch a company gives thirty-year employees.

The DSC, the Distinguished Service Cross, is the combat award; it's the one they give because it's been earned, and only after there has been an investigation, eyewitness statements taken, sworn testimony. It ranks just below the Medal of Honor.

Joe Brown knew his manners, so he accepted with gratitude; but he simply could not help saying, "There were a lot of other men in other helicopters at Bn Ca that night."

The two-star man smiled and said, "Although we are perfectly aware of that fact, we appreciate the fact you mentioned it. It only goes to show you earned the lesser decoration, too. The other men are also being suitably rewarded."

Humbly, Joe Brown nodded and expressed his thanks, then came to attention and saluted. It was over. The generals began talking to one another; March came over quickly and shook hands with Brown, envy like steel glimmers in his blue eyes. Then he excused himself hastily and went back to the generals where he was immediately accepted into the conversation. Bob Laya said, "I'll buy."

"I'll drink."

They went down to the club and got their drinks. That

118

is where she found him. Joe Brown stood slackly against the bar, head down, looking into the amber, swirling ice, when he became aware that someone had come up and stopped behind him, and had neither moved on nor said a word. Annoyed, Brown turned, and Jody said, "So this is what keeps you so busy."

Seeing her simply cut all Joe Brown's strings. With a dumb numbness he said, "Huh—"

"Do you know how many letters I've had from you in the past six weeks, Joe Brown?"

"Uh, ah, huh—"

"Exactly none. So I decided I'd better come over here and find out what the hell's going on."

Joe Brown looked at his wife, the brown eyes and hair and the fine bosoms, the legs; smelled her, and as she fell into his arms, Jody said, "Hi, Bob, see you around."

12

There was a layer of cumulus, broken, tops at about fifty-five hundred feet when the DC-10 arrived at Essenden Airport, Melbourne, Australia. The Ten broke through the clouds, mild turbulance, at about three thousand feet and turned on the downwind leg of the traffic pattern. Joe Brown woke when the ship bounced going through the clouds; he turned in his seat and looked at his wife and found her watching him. Then she pointed at the lighted signs and Joe Brown buckled up his seatbelt.

As a pilot, Joe automatically "helped" the pilots land the Ten, the way a driver sitting on the passenger side "brakes" a car he feels is being driven a bit too fast. Then they were down and reverse-thrust roared the engines and he relaxed.

Ten days.

They had ten days.

For ten days Joe Brown could dress in civilian clothes, go anywhere, do anything, and be with his wife the whole time. R&R. God damn, it was great!

They remained in their seats while all the people in a hurry crushed into the aisle and squeezed through the doors. The senior air hostess came hurrying along, and asked in her rich Aussie accent, "Is there anything wrong?"

"Just not in a hurry," Joe said, "letting the herd get on past."

Jody did not like the looks of her husband.

It was not the yellowish tinge to his skin so much, though she despised that; but her husband had been infected with malaria for so long—far longer than she remembered, for she had only known him a few years, and

120

been married to him less than one year. That was just part of the job, malaria, for a professional soldier who fought in the tropics, and forget all the propaganda on TV about how Project HOPE or something else had eradicated it on some island where no Americans, or American taxpayers, happened to live.

What she didn't like was how thin he was, a natural lightheavy when a young man, one seventy-five pounds and over, which made him a natural heavy at the age of forty-two, when nature thickened his bones and padded out the shoulder and back and thigh musculature. When she asked him, he said, "About one seventy, I guess; I don't remember last time Doc Elmore checked me. . . ."

And there were too many things he didn't want to talk about, and that not only upset her about his condition; it truly frightened her. . . .

Their courtship had not been an easy one: at first, they did not even particularly care for one another. Joe Brown had long been known for a rounder; he had always claimed, truthfully, he'd never been drunk, hungover, tired or sleepy or hungry, and very, very seldom horny. Though he had the decency not to say that in front of women like Jody Engel.

And then Ken Engel ceased to exist.

As a man, as an officer, as an army aviator.

He became a number.

Ken Engel was not even given the dignity of a name, but a number, six or ten or twenty-five, or if it had been a bad day for our side, perhaps he was number two hundred and eleven, in the lousy god damn *body count* issued in the daily press release handout at HQ, Saigon. It was as if he'd been a guy who went off the road and creamed himself in a car wreck on Easter weekend, trying to get back to the base on time.

Then, of course, it was open season on Jody Engel: all old Ken's buddies began coming around, anything we can do for you, honey? How about a drink, settle the old nerves. Most of the married officers who'd known Ken, or knew of him, were doing the cute little widow a big favor, since she was used to getting it regular when Ken wasn't overseas or off flying some colonels and generals on the air-taxi service, Stateside. Sure, Jody, baby, be glad to whip a little into you, honey, cheer you up, like a tranquilizer, make you sleep like a log.

Which was what made it all so very, very strange when Joe Brown called and asked if he could come by. She first said no, automatically, remembering his reputation, unmarried (oh, there had been a marriage, with a typical army or cop or fireman or politician ending to it; the guy away from home too much, especially nights, so a guy she worked with comes by . . .) and he'd been unmarried for quite a long time.

When she first told him no he could not come by, he made no protest, gave her no pitch, offered his sympathies, and rang off. A couple of days later she happened to encounter Colonel Eliot, whom she'd known most her life, on a trip down to Fort Bliss, to sign some papers. After they talked a bit, he asked if Brown had called her and she acknowledged Brown had and admitted she'd refused to see him. Eliot accepted it and asked no questions, but he had a curious expression on his face; and that made her ask why it was so special. Eliot had said, "I don't know that it's special at all, Jody . . . except Joe is the only living man who can tell you what really happened."

"Would you ask him to call me again?"

"No, Jody, I won't. He made the offer and you rejected it. If you want to talk to Joe Brown, you call him."

She could still remember the feeling of humiliation as she took down the address, and then tried to call and found he had no telephone listing. She finally wrote him a letter, to some tiny, hick village off up there on, or near, an Indian reservation in Arizona. He telephoned her a week later, and flew to Denver to see her.

To her complete surprise, he was the most gentlemanly of all the men who'd come to see her. He took her to dinner but made no effort to do her The Big Favor. And yet they did not seem to like one another very well. There was no eye-contact; they talked banally and inanely; once, even about how it is bad for the blood circulation to sleep with your ankles crossed. When he left after three days, his nights spent in a motel not even near her home, she was relieved, and perhaps she was still too numb—or afflicted with something she did not understand—for, when he told her how her husband had died, she chastised herself for not going to pieces as she thought she should have; because it was a gory, brutal and cowardly enough story. Some Viet slickships could have gotten Engel out if they'd had one single lousy pilot with the guts to go on in and make the honest effort. So Joe Brown had gone in himself, in a fixed wing old AD, a resurrected-from-mothballs old Navy fighter-bomber they had found a use for in Vietnam, and Joe Brown got Ken Engel out, but he was a cadaver when the medics unloaded him back at base.

Six weeks later, to her astonishment, Jody Engel saw Joe Brown standing on the corner waiting for the traffic light to change in downtown Denver. Without consciously willing herself to do so, she went up to him and touched his arm, and said something scintillatingly brilliant, like, "Remember me?"

He smiled and took off his cap and shook hands. He looked like cold meat some doctor was trying to Frankenstein. She discovered he was hospitalized out at Fitzsimmons for some ailment the doctors had not yet been able to diagnose. He looked so lousy she blurted, "How much do you weigh?" and he told her, "A hundred and thirty-seven and a half."

At first Jody was not sure of her motives, nor of where it seemed to be leading her, or Joe. She thought perhaps it was pure sympathy—"What you need is a good home-cooked meal!" Or perhaps a sense of indebtedness for what Joe had done about Ken, or tried to do. And she kept waiting for him to make the move, to do her The Big Favor—the biggest lie in the world:

"Aw, come on, honey, I'll only put the head of it in."

But he didn't make any moves, none whatever, except

123

that he seemed to enjoy himself enormously, just being in her company. They listened to records, watched the TV shows that did not gag either of them, and they talked; he was a superb raconteur, without knowing it, and almost all his stories were funny. None of them dealt with war or boxing, except a couple of funny ones about prizefighting when he was on leave, and down in Mexico.

The first time he ever kissed her was almost five months after she had seen him that day on the street in downtown Denver. He had asked her to go flying. He was simply dying to get his hands on an airplane again. They went off out into the country, searching around, until they found a crop-spray outfit with an old Piper Pacer sitting in the hangar. Joe got out and stood talking in the wind with the little guy who ran the outfit, showed him his military ratings, neglecting to evidence any medical certificate, took a twenty minute checkride—a couple of stalls, some turns, short touch-and-go landings in a gusting crosswind, with Joe settling her in there so the little feller had to look out the side window to make sure they were down.

Then she got into the airplane with him and they took off and it was beautiful, a word that came to have an especially particular meaning to them, later. And while they were up there flying over the Colorado farmlands east of the mountains, Joe started joking about initiating her into the Mile High Club. Jody did not understand, and Joe did not make it smutty enough for her to catch on, so finally he said, "How about an honorary membership?"

She agreed: he put his arm around her and kissed her.

From that point on Jody expected it to build and build, until she felt herself backed into a corner so she would be forced to a decision, about how far they would or could keep from going, so what she decided to do was never see him again.

But every time he called, she agreed.

She deliberately made dates, engagements, appointments for the nights she knew he could get free from the

124

hospital, so she would not have to lie or make thin excuses when he called. But when he called she said yes, and broke the other dates, or left the poor guys hanging, and never showed up for meetings.

Jody was no fool; she saw the same development in him. Now there was always eye-contact; they could not go near one another without touching. She was in love, and she knew that he was, too.

She kept waiting. For him to tell her what the doctors said at the hospital, for some declaration, for a question. None ever came; and finally on New Year's Eve, they had one other couple over and Jody said for all to hear, "I think tonight I'm going to get like I can't stand not getting what other women are getting."

At three o'clock the next morning they were on her couch, Joe sitting up, she stretched out along the length of the cushions in a pants suit, and she said, "Oh, God, Joe, I love you."

"And I love you, Jody."

For a long time he didn't say anything, and then with a terrible bitter edge in his voice he asked, "But what in the hell are we going to do about it?"

"I don't understand."

"I'm not quitting the army."

"I didn't ask you to quit."

"I won't be in the hospital much longer."

"Now I'm confused."

"The dumbutts finally figured out what's wrong with me. I'm eating myself alive. I got some kind of crazy infection. It was caused by a tiny shrapnel splinter I never even knew I took, in the gut. Some kind of pus cell full of enzymes or freak acids feed on it, so when I eat food it just goes on through my body like sand through a tin horn. I don't even get any nourishment from what I eat. Now they got it figured out, they can fix it. Once they fix it, I get shaped up, then if I pass my medical I'm an army aviator again."

He did not say the rest of it. He did not have to say more than he said. Vietnam consumed army, air force, navy, and marine corps aviators with the same insatiable senseless, mindless appetite that television used up people and talent and music and time and stories; with never a look backwards at the wreckage. When they become useless they drag the carcasses out of the way and throw something over them so they can't be seen; and spread quicklime and Lysol to kill the stink.

So they released him from Fitzsimmons, and fed him up and shaped him out and sent him in again, for his fourth tour, and he made it back; and it was all over now. That's what his bosses told him, and what the President promised the People; and then, the sons of bitches not only sent him back for the *fifth* time, they handed him an outfit that was in such rotten shape it was Big News: one part of the news media which had dedicated themselves to dishonoring and discrediting United States involvement in Vietnam tried to make heroes of the 504th, or was the proper word anti-heroes? The other portion of media, which somehow always ended up being called "spokesmen for the lunatic fringe and John Birchers" printed and broadcast a story much nearer the truth, but were already suspect because they used the wrong adjectives, and because they did not agree with the motor-mouthed spokesman whose speech at Michigan State University stated that "If you really understood what communism is, you'd fall on your knees and pray for us to be taken over by the communists."

Jody Brown knew what communism was, and is; she'd lost a husband to it, and saw what it had done to her new groom. She knew the only way she could have less luck was to have Joe Brown languishing in brainwashing undernourishment and physical torture in a North Vietnamese POW compound.

And what made her want to cry was, that it had become showboating. The lousy god damn war was over. We had surrendered; we had turned it over to them; a bunch of skinny little men, most of whom had no idea why they were there or what they were doing, except they'd been told by the VC and NVA conscriptors that

126

they could advance and have a chance, or certainly die if they retreated. So it all came to politics, on both sides; the guys in charge were involved at the ultimate level of The Games People Play.

At last Jody Brown understood why her husband had, at first, said he would not do another tour in Vietnam. It is senseless to continue to fight a war you have already admitted losing, just to make a bunch of catch-phrase jargon sound profound. Jody Brown even wondered if the leaders of the embattled nations had not entered into a secret agreement: that continuing the war was one solution to solving the increasingly serious problem of world overpopulation.

Why else did they keep that lousy god damn body count?

They were last to depart the DC-10 at Essendon and last to pass through customs and immigration and public health inspections; and being last also helped them avoid the hecklers, for the most part. A good many men on R&R from Vietnam chose Melbourne, and they were always in uniform when they landed, and were always met by a picket line with the usual slogans about baby-burners and grandma-rapers and the other complimentary jargon.

They first caught a taxi to the hotel where the army had reserved a room for them. After a bath and change, they found a bar, had a drink, walked a while on the lovely wide streets in the sunshine and had an early dinner.

The next day they went to a travel agency that had a booth set up in the hotel lobby and after a conference with the little man in charge, they arranged to rent a car for a tour of the Outback, as the boondocks or wilderness or country is called in Australia. As a born rancher, Joe had always wanted to see how they did it, and because he'd also always loved airplanes, Joe had read all of Nevil Shute's books; and that made him particularly eager to see places with names like Alice Springs, and

Coombargana, Wagga Wagga, Geelong and Warrnambool. It was only after checking the map that it came to Joe just how large a country Australia actually is and that getting into the real Outback meant about a half-day's run in a pretty fast airplane: Alice Springs, for example, was more that 2000 miles northwest of Melbourne, and the town was in the approximate center of the continent.

They settled for simply renting the car and touring through the Australian Alps, spending nights in high clean mountain air that reminded them of Arizona . . . some. . . .

But there was simply too much Vietnam stink still clinging to Joe Brown. Jody noticed that her husband was almost never without the odor of whisky on his breath, that he sometimes neglected to bathe and shave, that he smoked sometimes three packs of cigarettes a day, and then—

—The first time it happened, it so terrified Jody that she leaped from bed and ran cowering to a corner of the room, and pulled a huge oaken chair in front of her, a chair she found she could hardly lift with all her strength next day. She knew what nightmares were; she'd experienced Ken Engel's coming apart in the night a few times, after returning from Vietnam, and she'd had a bit of her own, after Ken's death. But she had never believed a man could have the kind of thing her husband had, the wide-eyed, clawing, throat-growling, cursing, screaming, lunging, endlessly-reliving scenes that finally left him exhausted and stinking of sweat so vile and slippery, that Jody could hardly stand to touch him when he finally came out of it and lay panting; and found the energy to make it into the toilet, to vomit hard, shuddering, rising into dry heaves, and then, again, so exhausted that when he got into the shower, he just sat there and let the water beat down on him. She had to stand by and regulate the water, because he seemed unaware when he was almost scalded, or when it ran pure cold, piped just below freezing from the Alpine streams.

She got almost no sleep the next night, because she lay there waiting for it to happen again; but Joe seemed all right and she finally dropped off. And the next night was fine, too; and not until the fifth night did it charge him again, hard. . . .

After he got himself cleaned up, it was almost daylight. They packed, went down and paid up, and drove to the hospital the army had set up for men on R&R out of Vietnam; and he turned himself over to the flight surgeon, with Jody at his side; because he did not remember much of it and she had seen it all.

The flight surgeon made a not very serious effort to hear the stories through, then wrote something on a pad and told Joe to pick them up at the pharmacy and follow the instructions precisely. Joe did, and of course found himself so loosely-laxed the rest of his leave he could not even make love to his wife, until he threw the pills away and finally they made it beautiful, the last night. Afterwards they talked until dawn began to creep a line across the ceiling of their room.

That was when Jody discovered what the nightmares were really all about: the Downhill Gang. As she listened to her husband talk, she realized he never said "the" men; he always said "my" men, or "my" boys. It was never the outfit, or the 504th, or the unit; it was "my" Downhill Gang.

That afternoon Jody said she wanted to do some shopping and left Joe sitting in the sun on the roof garden of the hotel, with a whisky in his hand. She went down and drove their little rented English car directly to the hospital and asked to see the same flight surgeon. The whole time she sat on the hard edge of the straightbacked chair and tried to explain her feelings, her fears, that she thought her husband was on the verge of identifying himself too closely with his men, if he had not already done so, the doctor smiled glassily. It was as though he were being polite and pretending to understand someone speaking a totally foreign language, of which he did not understand a word.

Finally, anger overcame Jody's concern. She rose to her feet and slammed her purse down on the doctor's desk. "Little man, you'd better stop dreaming of whatever it is that's got that stupid little smile on your face, and start listening to me!"

Stunned from his daydream, the doctor reared up in his chair and said, "Now see here, madame, ah, miss, uh, Mrs. Brown."

Jody had been around the army too long not to be aware of what clout meant, when and where and how to use it, if one must. She did not just lean on this grinny little man, she shoved him down, verbally. "I don't think you are quite aware of exactly who my husband is, Colonel Joseph Paul Brown. Perhaps, if you had learned to read by then, or at least understand photographs, you saw the picture of my husband and the man who was then President of the United States, in a little ceremony at the White House. And let me ask—have you ever heard of the Downhill Gang? They have even written a song about them, like the 'Ballad of the Green Berets.' Are you beginning to read me, major?"

Major Christensen was on his feet, and very nearly standing at the position of attention. "Mrs. Brown, I am dreadfully sorry—" He waved his arm around his office, which was about as *un*littered with paperwork as any office Jody Brown had ever seen, but Christensen persisted with the fiction, "—all this work. . . ."

He came around the desk, his blistery Scandinavian face set into a mask of sympathy and tried to take Jody's hand. "I actually do understand, perfectly; honestly, my dear—"

"Mrs. Colonel Joseph Paul Brown, if you please."

"Yes, of course! . . . Mrs. Brown, certainly I am aware of your husband's identity and reputation, and it was for precisely that reason I prescribed the treatment that I did." Christensen was so patently and obviously lying, Jody told him so, and said, "The only thing those damned pills did for him was give him another thing to worry about—being unable to make love."

130

Christensen's grin was so leeringly lewd that he might as well have said, "I'd be happy to oblige you, my dear," and Jody almost hit him.

Hastily, Christensen backed away, and got the desk between himself and this viciously angry woman, and Jody saw his face as his mind searched around for and finally came up with another lie, and the doctor said, "Mrs. Brown, you must believe me, the, ah, condition you mentioned is, ah, temporary. After a few weeks of treatment, I'll prescribe another ah, less powerful compound and—"

"A few more weeks. Buster, you belong in a rubber room somewhere. In a few more weeks my husband will have been back on duty with his unit in Vietnam for a few weeks."

"Oh, well, then—"

"No, you don't. I want you to put my husband under the care of a psychiatrist."

"And ruin his career? You can't be serious."

"I am absolutely serious, major. I happen to have been the widow of an army aviator before I married Colonel Brown. The army took my first husband and used him up and shipped me a pile of rotted guts in a rubber bag. I think my present husband is too much man for those gook sons of bitches to kill, ever; but I don't want *him* shipped home with unfocused eyes and spit dribbling down his chin."

"I simply can't accept the responsibility of doing what you want, Mrs. Brown, without further personal examination of your husband."

"So it's your career, not his, that you're really worried about."

"There are certain formalities, Mrs. Brown; actually regulations, which must be complied with. Unless a man is a raving lunatic, there is simply no possible way that I could propose psychiatric treatment, even an interview with our psychiatrist." By the time he finished, Christensen was pleading, and Jody believed he was probably telling the truth.

131

"If you had seen him have that last nightmare, you'd certify him all right."

"Probably so, but—I wasn't—"

"All right, I'll have him back here in an hour. If you are not here, I promise that my husband will put you on report." Jody leaned forward on the desk and Christensen stepped back a pace. She said, "And when we come in this time, Major, try to pay attention to what my husband tells you, instead of ogling my legs and acting as though you'd lost something down the front of my dress!"

Christensen's face went from blistery to positively scarlet, and he looked down at his shoes as Jody left. That was the last she ever saw of him, for when she returned to the hotel she did not find Joe on the roof-garden of the hotel, she found him in their room, packing.

He smelled strongly of whiskey, but he was not drunk. He kissed her extra long, and held her close to him for a long, long time. Then, as he finished putting a last few items into his toilet kit, he pointed to a yellow sheet of paper lying on the dresser.

Jody picked it up and began to read, and then tears blurred out the words. She went into the bathroom and wiped her eyes with tissue and closed the door and leaned against the sink and read it, all the way through.

Emergency orders. The 504th had been called back into action two weeks earlier than anticipated. Huge NVA buildup along the DMZ; intelligence reports indicate major offensive directed at Quang Tri province, directly south of the DMZ, with anticipated major push on into the next province southward, Thua Thien.

Jody did not even try to hold him, to tell him of the appointment with Major Christensen. She leaned against the sink and cried that silent, shuddering, gut-tearing way she cried; and listened to the last sounds of getting ready made by her husband as he completed packing his gear. She saw him off at Essenden, and later that same night caught a Quantas flight to Los Angeles, and a Continental to Phoenix. While she unlocked the door of the house in Pinetop, far across the sea in Southeast Asia, her husband was at the controls of a *Bell UH-1 Huey Hog* gunship, his fourth mission of the day.

13

Marston stood trembling with fury and Brown let him soak in the rage, and then, Brown said, "Well?"

"Because I can't make helicopters fly with vulture droppings and wishful thinking. We haven't had a delivery of spares for ten days, and this outfit has flown more than fifty missions and I've cannibalized every hangar-queen we've got. If I had a proper machine shop and the raw materials I'd *make* the parts, but all I've got is a drawer-full of back order requisitions and a big ration of shit from you."

"I don't want alibis, I want aircraft aloft; and by God if you can't get them into the air, I'll find a man who can."

"I'd like that. Do it *yesterday* if you can. But let me tell you one thing, Colonel, the next maintenance officer you get in here had better be Jesus Christ himself if you want flyable helicopters made of this junk we've got now."

"All right, Marston, you've made it plain enough. Put in your request for transfer and I'll approve it. Dismissed."

Brown became aware of Walker's unblinking stare after Marston stormed from the room. Without rancor, Brown said, "What's eating you?"

"That performance."

"Hell, I was just trying to goose him up a little."

"Goose him up a little? You talked to him like—hell, I can't think of a comparison. You were on him like stink in a slit-trench. And all he is, is the best god damn helicopter maintenance officer in the *world*!" Walker got to his feet and threw his arms wide in a gesture of utter helplessness. Then he turned to Brown and said, "Let me give you a short bulletin, boss. Marston's time is up; it was up nine weeks ago; he could have gone out. He stayed because of what you were making out of the 504th, the Downhill Gang. He could, he damned well *could*, be gone from here twenty-four hours from now. I don't mean off this base. I mean he could be *gone*. And you know what else he *could* do. Walk into Bell Helicopter Company's office, sit down, take a pen in hand, and sign a contract that would make his current wages look like those of a wetback field hand's."

Walker turned and walked away and then faced Brown again, and he said, "You can fire me, run me out, send me to stockade; but Skipper, I'm telling you right now, you'd better let up. If you don't, you're going to crack wide open."

"That's good advice which I don't need." Brown got to his feet and put his hands on his desk and leaned forward, snapping the words out, "Don't ever try talking to me like that again, in that tone of voice, with that kind of buddy-buddy attitude. You got that, Captain?"

"Yes, sir." Walker's face went red with angry embarrassment.

Feeling assy, wrong, and almost unable to keep himself from acting like a first-class heel, Brown shook his head as he sat down and breathed deeply. "Hell, Dale, I'm sorry; forget what I said, and how I said it."

"All right." Walker returned to his chair.

Brown picked up a sheet of paper on his desk and as he did so, he could not keep his hand from trembling. It was the daily summary of casualties, a crappy-mouthed Madison Avenue euphemism for the body count. Brown passed the paper to Walker. "You verified this?"

"Yes, sir."

"Then get the lousy god damn thing off to Saigon. We wouldn't want March to be caused any delay. Christ, I've never seen a man who can grin so widely and stick his chest out so far when he talks about the deads and maimed and missing."

135

Walker nodded. "I attended one of those sessions, and that once will last me all the rest of my life."

"What shape are we in?"

"Not good, except that we have so few choppers flyable that our manpower factor isn't critical." Walker paused, and in his manner Brown read the young man's hesitancy. Brown said, "Forget what I said. We can talk. We always could and we still can. I just had a case of the butt a while ago."

"Why do you still insist upon running 504 without an executive officer? Christ, Colonel, in the beginning it was understandable. Nobody thought you could do any more with this outfit than the last guy who tried, and got shipped; and nobody wanted to come in with you and ride the skids down with you. But all these papers cross my desk, it's my job, and I know you've had applications for the XO job from some outstanding men."

Brown didn't look into Walker's eyes when he replied, "I know. Some of them are so good, well, it's hard to make a decision. Like making a choice between Pete Chatam and Ernest Crawford. I don't need to tell you that Lea is not even in the running; he's March with handles, an opportunist. He'd come in here and work like a slave until I left, then take over and make sure word got around that without him, I'd have fallen on my ass if he hadn't worked thirty hours a day and held my hand to keep things going; and the next time we met at the club or a ballgame back Stateside he wouldn't recognize me."

"What about Fugate?"

"You're reading my mind, Walker. That's who I want, if we accept anyone."

"Please, Colonel, get him in here. He's not a glory hunter. He's the most outstanding management and personnel man in Southeast Asia, and a real expediter." Walker got up and came over to Brown's desk. "OK, sir?"

"I'll think about it. Probably I will. We'll discuss it tomorrow. What else now?"

"That Lieutenant Harmon thing is still hanging fire."

Brown got to his feet and paced the office like a scorpion in a glass jug, shaking his head, his left hand jerking nervously.

"Walker, this has got to be the most fucked up, confused, irrational, incredibly mismanaged, stupidly— By God, I'll tell you, when I first saw *that* report I *could not believe* it."

"Nor could I, sir. I thought someone was trying to run a fast one past us. But I investigated it personally, and it's true."

Brown's shoulders slumped and again he shook his head. 'You know, it's gotten to where we can't even fight the war any longer, not effectively, even if we had the gear, which 504 is not getting, for some reason. But if we had it *all*, we'd still be so enmeshed in these lousy *employee-relations* problems we'd still be at about seventy percent effectiveness, instead of shoving ahead fullballs." Brown sighed. "You looked into it?"

"Yes, sir."

"And nine black soldiers have signed that—whatever it was—petition, complaint?—against a *black* officer?"

"They claim he's too hard on them, expects too much of them, rides them too hard."

"OK, to hell with it, ship them, all nine. I'm not going to let this get complicated. They can raise all the hell they want, call me a racist, write letters to Dick Gregory and their congressmen, any damned thing they want, but ship them, tonight. Before one of them gets stoned on something and tries to frag Harmon, or some smartass white in the unit tries to frag him so the blacks get blamed."

Walker went to the telephone and got the movement in motion, and when he hung up, Brown said, "I want a Letter of Commendation, without the combat valor V, presented to Harmon tomorrow. We've got to protect him and also let him know those other nine shits didn't beat him. You get him in for a personal interview, too; and let him know what the deal is."

Walker said, "There is the best example I can give

you why you should issue one other order tonight, sir. This is the kind of thing Fugate could handle so smoothly the air wouldn't even ripple."

Brown turned his back and walked away, looking down at the floor. After a long moment, he asked, "Is Fugate a tiger? I mean, is he one of the fire-eaters who likes to jump into a gunship alone at night and roar off with his scarf flying in the breeze and shoot up free-fire zones?"

"Quite the opposite. You read his file: he started as an intelligence officer and performed brilliantly, but that is a dead-end specialty, like we are in aviation, unless we make a point to learn other skills, further our education, round out our backgrounds. Why the hell do you think those forty-five- and fifty-year old colonels go through paratroop jump school, and apply for flight training? Like the Navy; you can't command an aircraft carrier, or a task force, unless you are a rated naval aviator. I read where Admiral Halsey went through Pensacola when he was *fifty-four years old*. He saw the war with Japan coming, and knew it would be a sea war, and he knew he'd never command a carrier or anything more than a line ship unless he got wings. Fugate's the same way; he didn't want to retire after thirty-years service as a light colonel, or with the eagle if he got the breaks. You see guys in our service the same; all they want to do is fly airplanes, so they do nothing else, and go out on half-pay as majors or sometimes lieutenant colonels after twenty years service; because they've done nothing to broaden their skills and knowledge and abilities, so they get passed over for promotion and retired out."

"So what you're telling me is that Fugate is a flyer, but really a man on the way up."

"Yes, sir, but not the kind, if I may say so, like Colonel March, who does not care whose face he steps on making the climb."

"All right, get him in."

"Thank you, sir."

"Why thanks?"

"Because when Lieutenant Colonel Fugate arrives, I'll only have three jobs instead of four."

Brown laughed. "I guess you don't get much sleep, do you?"

"Enough, and now I'll get more; probably a whole hour every night."

Brown had a thought come to him with the force of a bronc kicking him in the guts. He looked at Walker for a long time, and finally he had to ask him, "Have you ever thought the reason I did not want an exec was because I did not wish to share the glory, to share what I had made of 504?"

The question and the implication, Brown saw, so shocked and dismayed Walker that it made Brown have to turn away and blow his nose. After a moment, Walker said, "Colonel Brown, with the exception of my own father, I have never known a man I respect more, and thought was more a man, than you. My father was incapable of such behavior. Just as you are."

"Well, OK, now what the hell else business have we got to clean up here."

"In order of priorities, Colonel, you must go see Major Marston and do whatever you have to to keep him."

Brown nodded.

"Second, we have to get spares. Some place, somewhere, somehow, we have got to get spares; and I mean steal them, if that's what it takes."

Brown returned to his desk and sat down, saying, "I don't think that will be necessary. If it is, I will personally lead the raid."

Brown picked up his telephone and got Marston on the line. "Bring all those returned requisitions and back orders to my office, if you are not too busy making out your request for transfer. . . ."

Marston said, "Aw, hell, Colonel. . . ."

"Try to get over right away, Ray. I think we may have solved the problem. Of course, our young fireeater here, Walker, suggests we hijack—"

"I'll lead the raid."

"I've already taken that job."

Marston arrived with a large folder which he spread out on the desk. As Brown had suspected—and mentally kicked himself in the skull for not catching on earlier—more than ninety percent of the requisition refusals and requests for back orders were signed by the same man. Brown reached for the telephone and called his communications chief. "Rig up a radio-telephone patch and get me through to—" and Brown mentioned the name of the two-star man who'd been in Paulson's office the day Brown had been awarded the two decorations. Brown told his CC, "I want you to keep trying until you find him; his office, his quarters, the embassy, the presidential palace, the senior officers' club, the Caravel, or some goddam whore-house, but I want to talk to that man today."

"My God, Colonel," Marston said, banging his hand against his forehead, "I should have spotted it myself."

"You've been too busy; so has Walker." Smiling drily, Brown said, "Fugate wouldn't have missed it, would he?"

Walker shook his head.

To Brown's astonishment, the two-star man returned the call in ten minutes. He was extremely friendly, but just a slight edge of tonelessness crept into his voice when he mentioned he hadn't heard much from the Downhill Gang lately.

"Which is precisely why I've called you, General."

"Yes."

"We're getting the screws put to us in Saigon."

There was a considerable pause, then the two-star man said, "Brown, you rather disappoint me. That's a complaint I hear constantly from field commanders. I had been absolutely persuaded that you were a man of great initiative and personal prowess; and that the last thing you would ever resort to is some kind of alibi blaming those so-called rear-echelon-bastards in Saigon."

"General, I would not have thought of calling you, for the very reasons you stated, except that—"

"Come on, Brown, what is it? If you've got a gripe, let's hear it."

Brown told him.

The two-star man's voice was like rusty steel across stone. "You can, of course, prove this?"

"I have the copies of them on the desk in front of me. General, to be absolutely candid, and vulgar, someone is fucking over us to make us look bad. We want it stopped. We want it stopped because we want to do what we are out here to do: fight."

There was another long pause, and then, the two-star man said a very strange and peculiar thing which Brown did not understand at all, until that afternoon. The two-star man said, quietly, as though speaking personal thoughts aloud, "It is very disquieting how little odds and ends and bits and pieces that seem to make no sense whatever, suddenly, all come together to make a crystal-clear pattern . . . when the missing piece is found."

Uncertainly, Brown said, "Yes, sir. . . ."

Briskly, the two-star man said, "If I do not make contact with you myself, an officer which I delegate to handle this matter will be in touch with you in . . . let's say no more than two hours. Is there anything else, Colonel Brown?"

"No, sir, I just appreciate—"

"Yes, yes, quite so. Good afternoon, sir."

Joe Brown put the telephone down and sat back, dripping with sweat. He told Marston and Walker about the end of the conversation they could not hear. Brow wrinkled, Walker said, "I don't get this. There's a piece missing. Or at least something he didn't tell you."

"Sure," Brown said, "But I didn't make much sense of it either."

Marston said, "I did."

"What?" Brown asked, as did Walker.

"The general knows who that guy is." Marston indicated the stack of requisitions and back orders. "He recognized the name, and when he did, he knew the motive. That's what he meant by the bits and pieces falling together."

Joe Brown looked up at Ray Marston and, to himself,

141

predicted that the maintenance officer would some day, if he chose to go that route, be president and chief executive officer of Bell Helicopter Company. Or any other outfit he chose to go with.

Brown shot a look at Walker, but the captain was already on his feet and headed for the door, saying, "I'll find out soon as I can who he is. CID can probably find out quicker than anyone; I mean get a call through to Saigon HQ and have one of their men take a look at his file."

Marston said, "You'd better get hold of your comm chief and get yourself lost, except for calls from the general or his representative."

Brown grinned as he lifted the receiver and told CC, "I'm on a test flight unless that two-star man calls, or someone you can verify as his representative. Any rockets that come in from Paulson or March, just deflect them off into the boondocks, and send a runner to find me if the other call comes through."

They went down to the maintenance hangar and drank coffee and Marston indulged a habit that until now Brown did not know of; the maintenance officer dipped snuff; that is to say, he took a tiny pinch and placed it between his lower lip and gum on the left side. Twenty minutes and two cups of coffee later, Walker came strolling into the hangar, cap on the back of his head, hands in his pockets, whistling "The Ballad of the Downhill Gang." With exaggerated lack of concern, he poured a cup of coffee. Marston moved his weight from one leg to the other, back and forth, like a child about to wet his pants. Brown made himself exhibit an unconcern equaling Walker's, and had the captain pour him another cup of coffee, and then Walker couldn't hold it any longer.

Grinning, he said, "Hey, guess what I found out?"

"Santy Claus ain't for real," Brown said.

"What-what?" Marston demanded.

"Guess—now you get just one guess apiece—who Colonel March's son-in-law is."

Colonel Joe Brown's entire body went rigid, and
142

though he could not see himself, he felt his whole Indian-dark body go white with rage, and between clenched teeth, he said, "Dale—"

"Just another lil' ol' Texas Aggie, sho nuff, and married to Geraldine, usually called Jeri, Bedwell, nee March."

Brown felt himself shaking so hard he had to grab his coffee cup with both hands, and missed, and the thick white crockery dropped to the floor and smashed; and, in a blind rage, he kicked the largest piece clear across the hangar. He shook his head, turning to Walker; he thought he might be crying but he was not sure. He took Walker's elbows and held him fast. "No, no, Dale," Brown said, shaking his head, feeling sick.

Walker's assumed gaiety vanished, and he said, "Yes, it is true, Colonel, the lousy sons of bitches, and that's not all. Get this, just get a fucking load of this one!"

He jerked free of Brown's grasp. "I got hold of Fugate. He nosed around. March has been after your job since you went on R&R. Paulson didn't dare give it to him, not so soon after they pinned the tin on your chest, so they got up the little deal. March's son-in-law got transferred into the slot he's got, and no spares for the Downhill Gang. The 504 doesn't get into the air any more, time for a change of command, you dig?"

Brown looked around the wide, open hangar, out the vast door into the crushing afternoon glare. He looked at Walker, he turned and looked at Marston, and then not really speaking personally to either man, Brown said, "But we are fighting a war." He jerked his left hand toward a Hog awaiting repairs. "The only reason those deadly sons of bitches exist is to make war, to help our men on the ground to kill the enemy, to protect our infantrymen. . . ."

Bitterly, with a grinding, absolute, utter bitterness, Walker said, "That's where you're all fucked up, Colonel, sir. The war's over, we're pulling out, so now's the time to make reputations, to pull the old semper fi, as the Marines call it: *fuck you, pal, I got mine*! It's just that

143

simple. March was going to cash in on your accomplishments."

"Only if he can," Brown said. "Get the Blue Canoe ready, we're going to Saigon." He turned to Marston, "Ray, you are relieved of your command. I can no longer use the best man in the business."

Marston's mouth opened and closed and he tried to speak, but Brown held up a hand and stopped him. "I want a promise from you."

"If I can."

"Get out of this shithole country today, if you can." Brown turned to Walker. "We'll all three go in to Saigon. You take Ray directly to Fugate. If he's the expediter you say he is, he can have Ray on a MAC flight out of Tan Son Nhut tonight." Brown licked his lips. "Go tell Doc Elmore he is also relieved. I no longer want or need a flight surgeon dedicated to keeping pilots flying. March can have 504, he can fold it and stuff it up his ass, and it will *be* a Downhill Gang by the time he finishes with it, by the time it finishes with him."

Walker took Brown's arm gently. "Colonel, you can't do this. Once you think about it, you won't *allow* yourself to do it. It's positively disgraceful. God damn it, it's dishonorable!"

"You just get that Cessna ready, son." Brown went away from there.

14

Brown rode the back seat of the Blue Canoe, with Doc Elmore beside him. Walker flew in the left seat forward, and Marston rode beside him. In the baggage compartment the gear of the two relieved officers was stowed. There was not much of it; both were combat men; they did not bring trunks and valises, suitcases and an endless number of B-4 bags with them to Vietnam, because they had come to work, not sightsee and collect souvenirs.

Brown had little to say, except to explain to Elmore why he was going out. Elmore accepted it with the calm logic that personified the man. He was quiet, tough, lanky; with a pockmarked face, intense eyes, quiet and calm; he always seemed to be waiting for something, usually a lie or a con job, some airman tried to put on him at sickcall. More than once Joe Brown had thought what an excellent cop Elmore would have made, had he chosen that profession instead of medicine.

They joined the traffic pattern at Tan Son Nhut, and on the downwind leg saw one of those sickening tragedies of war in the air: over the radio there suddenly came a frantic call from a Douglas A-4 Skyhawk, an aircraft-carrier-based-subsonic jet fightplane, this flown by a Marine. The pilot's calm but fear-constricted voice declared an emergency and asked for a straight-in landing. The tower cleared everything off, putting the other aircraft into holding patterns and the Skyhawk came in. Watching from his side window, Brown saw the airplane's nose wheel was not down and locked, though both mains appeared to be. Out on the runway, two firetrucks ran at top speed laying down a strip of foam.

The Skyhawk came in low and "dirty"—that is, with

flaps and wheels and speedbrakes extended to slow the airplane's speed as much as possible, and the pilot was good. He put the mains down right on the runway numbers, and kept the stick back in his gut, holding the nose high, until the forward speed diminished and the nose began to lower, because that's how the center of gravity was built into the airplane. The nose lowered farther and farther, and in a touch of sparks hit the runway, then a vast shower of foam made a double rooster-tail as the nose of the airplane plowed through the foam the trucks had laid down.

"Son of a bitch!" Walker shouted with glee, "what a pilot. He's made—"

And silently Joe Brown was thinking the same—

When the left main gear collapsed and the airplane fell off on its right wing, and began to cartwheel down the runway, bursting the fuel cells, metal striking sparks off to the side of the foam strip; and then, the airplane exploded, and the calm voice of the tower operator began directing traffic to alternate runways while the ground crewmen cleaned up the mess.

The two-star man's car met them and they rode straight to his office. In an outer chamber sat Paulson and March, and March's son-in-law, Bedwell. In chairs on the other side of the room sat three more men: Fugate; Major Holder, the new flight surgeon; and Major Paseman, who was Marston's relief.

The moment Brown entered the room Paulson rose to his feet and came at him, chomping his cigar. He opened a side door and holding it, Brown entered and Paulson followed. They were alone in a small office. There were papers about, even a page in a typewriter; obviously the room's occupant had been hurriedly vacated for the purpose of this conference.

Immediately the door closed, Paulson whirled on Brown. "God-*damn*, Joe, why'd you go over my head like this? You've got me up to my neck in a tub of shit, and depending upon what goes on in there with the General, I swear to you now, I'll break you."

146

"You'll have the chance, General, because it's all about to get spread out like a chart on a table, for everyone to see."

"Why the hell couldn't you have come to me if you thought March and Bedwell were putting the blocks to you? God-*damn*, Joe, we were at the Point together; we go back a long ways, forever!"

"Because I didn't—don't trust you, General. You and I have never made it together, not since the day you decided to climb into the ring with me and whip me and become captain of the boxing squad, way back then. And I kicked the crap out of you, KO'd in just over one minute of the first round. You've never forgiven me for it."

"That's ridiculous. That was . . . hell, almost twenty-five years ago."

"Then why wouldn't you see me, personally, as is the custom and the courtesy, when an officer comes in to take over a new command?"

Paulson looked away. "I was busy that day."

"I don't believe it. I think you did not have the guts to face me, and tell me I'd been given the 504, and that at last you would have your revenge . . . because you *expected* me to fail. By God, you wanted me to fail!"

"I warn you against making any such accusation outside this room, Brown."

Brown stared at the man, and told Paulson the most contemptible comparison that he found in his mind: "You know what's wrong with you base-force bastards? You're scared. You're running with your eyes watching back over both shoulders, and you know what you're afraid of? The lousy god damn fucking news people. You've run with them and from them, and kissassed them so much you've come to practice incest just like they do. All any of you bastards want out of this war now is a reputation. You and your god damn pitiful imitation of Curt LeMay, your pose and posture and style, photogenic. You puke, you lousy god damn incest-practicing puke."

Paulson bit his cigar in half and that portion outside

147

his mouth fell to the floor. He almost choked on the other half, and spat it out. In a fury that made his voice rise to a half-scream, he shouted, "I am a *General* in the United States Army! You can't talk to me like that!"

"And I am a Colonel in the United States Army, and when I'm in the right, I'll talk to a dog like he's a hound, and I don't care how many stars he's got pinned on his tailored blanket." Brown turned toward the door, but Paulson grabbed his arm, "Joe, Joe, listen to me."

Brown stopped and faced Paulson. "Joe, god damn it, I had nothing to do with this, absolutely nothing."

"But you just reminded me, you're the General; and everything under your command is your responsibility. Look what your fucking news-media boys tried to have done to Medina and Oran Henderson. They went up the side of your rear-echelon bastards' heads so the whole army over-reacted, filed charges against everybody in sight, good old fuck-your-brother week. Tell me that's not incest."

Paulson started to say something, but there was a knock at the door, and Brown seized the opportunity to break off the talk by opening the door at once. March stood there, and he was not his usual gleamingly-polished self. His lightweight nonregulation blouse, cut to fit his fine figure, was soaked with sweat clear to the waist. Hesitantly, he started into the room, but Brown blocked his way. March's voice pleaded, "Joe, just for a minute, I've got to talk to you."

Brown shook his head, staring March down; then Joe pushed past him and heard March telling Paulson, "But, sir, I—" and then he was out of earshot.

They waited twenty minutes. Brown introduced himself to Fugate, Paseman and Holder; he told them they could return to the aviation HQ if they wished and he would meet them there, then they would return to the airport and fly back to 504 base. Paseman and Holder agreed and left, but Fugate said, "I've uncovered a bit more chicanery that we might offer in evidence, so I'll stick around, if that suits you?"

Brown nodded. "You're my executive officer. What have you got?"

"Oh, just a little something from Australia that might come in handy if we need it."

"Australia?" Brown looked at him. "How the hell—Why—"

Fugate grinned. "Intelligence work tends to make a man overlook *no* possibility. Do you know a flight surgeon named Christensen?"

"I don't think so."

"Yes, you do; you just don't remember him. He was the guy you talked to in Melbourne."

"Sure, the redfaced creep. Really fixed me up. Gave me some tranquilizers so strong I couldn't even make it with Jody."

"Did you know your wife had gone to see him alone?"

"What?"

Just then the door of the two-star man's office opened and a 1/Lt aide said, "Colonel Brown and party, please."

They went inside. It did not take long. The two-star man already knew the story from Brown's telephone call. Now Joe and his officers laid out the evidence, including —to Joe's surprise—some extensive records of inventories on hand at the time Bedwell had returned Marston's requisitions for back order. The spares had been on hand. Fugate also showed copies of records that on several occasions when identical parts had been ordered by 504 and another unit, and the spares were on hand, Bedwell had returned 504's requisition and sent the spares to the other unit.

The two-star man said very little. He asked a question or two from time-to-time, precise questions that required exact answers, which Brown and his men, frequently Fugate, were able to supply without hesitation.

The two-star man gestured to his aide and the 1/Lt began gathering the papers. "Put them in the safe." The two-star man got to his feet, shook hands with Brown and the others, said, "You need not concern yourselves with this any longer, unless there is another delay in getting

149

spares, or any other items you need. I'll take care of it from here on."

The aide ushered them out, and Brown was surprised to find that Paulson, March, Bedwell were not there, awaiting their turns before the general.

Back at 504, Brown discovered that huge Skycrane helicopters had delivered everything that Marston had been unable to get for weeks. Paseman dove right into the work, and far into the night he had his men still at it, getting the Hogs ready to fly. Brown had the new flight surgeon in for an interview: "Do you know, have you heard, what the policy is—rather, what it was in this unit?"

"Yes, sir."

"Do you approve?"

"I suppose the policy itself tends to prove itself, sir; it works."

"That was not the question."

"Then, no, sir; to be candid, I do not approve."

"Why not?"

"I simply do not believe that every man who comes to sick call is a malingerer, unless he has a visible compound fracture or some similarly, and easily, identifiable ailment."

"You mean there are such things as pains in the lower back, of undetermined origin, which really can disable a man so much he should be grounded."

"Yes, sir, I do."

Brown made no immediate reply. He swung back and forth in his swivel chair, eyes roaming the ceiling, until he became aware that Holder had become rather nervous. Brown said, "I beg your pardon, Major Holder. Do you drink?"

"Bourbon if you have it."

Brown got out his supply and poured the doctor's shot and an Old Parr for himself, then sat down. They lifted glasses toward one another, and sipped.

Brown asked, "Doctor, have you ever participated in

150

organized athletics? I mean on a relatively high level of competition?"

For a moment, Holder did not say anything, then he asked, "May I be permitted to anticipate you? Or state what I believe you are getting at?"

Brown nodded.

"Colonel, you must know that your reputation is very widely known, which means that certain beliefs, philosophies you have are also well known. What you're getting at is this: if a man has enough desire, he can overcome tremendous odds, including pain; if it means enough to him, personally, for whatever reason or motive, then he can do things actually beyond his capacity. Am I correct in anticipating you?"

"Exactly. But you don't agree?"

"Of course I agree, Colonel, within certain limitations."

"Such as?"

"First, motive. The motive must be of such great and consuming importance to the man, or the men, that they will extend themselves beyond any reasonable human capability to achieve the goal. It comes very simply to this: just what it is worth to the individual; the sacrifices he is willing to make; how bad he really wants it."

Joe Brown nodded, remembering; that's what they'd said about him, back when he was in top form and before his left hand turned faithless and started breaking. It was the same kind of thing they said about Lombardi, and Bear Bryant, and that little guy who coached the Celtics; that they actually took an unfair advantage over opponents, because they simply wanted to win that bad; like Wooden's kids at UCLA. They seemed to have grown some extra layer of unbending and impenetrable hide, so that losing was simply no longer a part of their make-up. That's what Joe Brown had done with the Downhill Gang.

But as he talked to Doctor Holder, something that had been eating at the back of Joe Brown's mind began coming into focus. He asked Holder, "What is your personal thinking on the subject?"

151

Holder's face reddened slightly, and Brown said at once, "I don't want any holding back, and don't be afraid to express yourself freely."

"I think it's all rather silly."

"Rather red than dead, huh?"

"Of course not, Colonel; I didn't mean that at all."

"Live coward rather than dead hero; he who fights and runs away, all that horseshit?"

"No, sir, I do not mean those at all. It is not my personal philosophy, nor is it my professional ethic, to condone or encourage malingering. I simply think it is both unnecessary and unwise to make men fly airplanes when there is a questionable—"

"You're a book man."

"That's what the book is for." Holder took another sip of his bourbon. "Colonel, may I say something, be absolutely candid?"

"You may."

"Out here we are not engaged in a football game or a prizefight. I think it is unfair to the men themselves, as well as medically unethical, to certify a man for flight duty when he is obviously not fit for it."

"You'd be in a hell of a fix if you ever got assigned to an infantry outfit, wouldn't you, Doc?"

Holder nodded his head in agreement. "I think I would have to resign. I don't think I'm capable of patching up maimed men, and then sending them back for a final butchering . . . particularly now."

"Particularly now?" Brown made a question of Holder's last words.

Holder gestured helplessly with both hands. "It's over. We're pulling out. We've given it over to them." He took a sip of his bourbon, finishing it. "Do you know, Colonel Brown, there really isn't any need for men of your breed in Vietnam any longer? You hardnosed winners? It's all just politics now, and perhaps an opportunity for the tigers, the outright killers, to get in some last high body counts."

Brown got to his feet and stuck out his hand, and as

they shook, he told Holder, "Thanks for coming over, Doc. Get this straight. You run your department. I won't interfere, ever; except in one way; no—make that in two ways. Fugate is not to fly except enough to maintain his proficiency and draw flight pay; and I will not be grounded."

For a long moment, Holder hesitated, and then he agreed, reluctantly. Brown walked him to the door, and they parted and Brown went on over to the maintenance hangar. He found Paseman up to his ears in grease and engine oil, called him aside, and said, "You'd better knock off now. Let your men get some rest, and do the same yourself."

"But, sir, we've still only got four ships in top shape, really combat ready."

"Then we'll just have to scramble four if the chime rings. I don't like to work with my officers this way, Pase, but I will if I have to. Knock off for the night. That's an order."

"Yes, sir."

Brown went to the club and had a drink. On the juke, over and over, because many replacement officers had come into the unit now, Donny-Joe Ainsworth's recording of "The Ballad of the Downhill Gang" played over and over and over, and each time it started again, Joe Brown felt himself becoming sadder and tireder, until he finally just signed his tab and left a half-drink unfinished on the bar.

He went to his room and lay down on his bunk, forearm across his eyes. The conference with Holder had not been a good thing for Joe Brown; or it had been the best thing that had yet happened to him in Vietnam. He could not decide. He lay there and he thought, and sometime during the night he dropped off to sleep. He did not wake until Walker rapped on his door next morning and entered, with the new clerk, Louderback, coming along behind with a tray loaded with coffee pot, toast, cream and sugar and a single tiny one-ounce bottle of brandy. Brown noticed that this morning there were three cups on the tray, and Walker said, "I've asked Colonel Fugate to join us."

Brown nodded and took the cup after Walker put in a quarter-ounce of brandy, a touch of cream and a few grains of sugar, then filled it with steaming coffee. Fugate entered and after they were all set, they conferred.

With a smile, Brown asked Fugate, "What do your spies report from Saigon? Have they run March and Bedwell up with the flag to see if they'll hang straight or crooked?"

"Very curious, that. Neither Paulson nor March have been relieved or transferred. Bedwell was moved to another department, where he shuffles papers concerned with such items as toilet paper and pro-kits."

Brown shrugged. "How's the saying go, about wheels of justice?"

Fugate didn't say anything, but he did not seem to agree, while Walker finished the axiom and reckoned there wouldn't be enough dust to ship home after the two-star man finished with those bastards. Fugate didn't say anything except, "Excellent coffee."

An hour later, the klaxon went; the flight crews scrambled, and the Downhill Gang was back into the war again.

They flew all day.

The NVA had moved into Quang Tri Province south of the DMZ, in great force; three hard, stiff probing punches of at least regimental size, well-armed and mobile, and seemingly equipped with three or four million goddamn AK-47s. It appeared to Brown that gunships were going down in flames everywhere he looked, until it seemed that all angles of his vision were filled with dying Hogs, and among them were two from Downhill Gang.

Brown managed to get down and rescue two door-gunners, but both the pilots were dead and one of the other gunners dead. The other man vanished, until as he pulled his ship up to get out and away, he saw three NVA soldiers shoving and prodding a captured American along a jungle path.

154

For a moment, Brown had the urge to turn his guns on them; he had the real urge to do so to the degree that he swung his Hog around and brought his guns to bear. It would be a favor to the captured man, Brown was sure; but he could not bring himself to press the trigger. He swung the ship aside and fired a rocket past the men, and hoped in the exploding confusion the American would escape, but he had no real hope of that.

All the way back to base all he could think of was the gunner being led by a rope around his neck through the villages and hamlets of Quang Tri, dirty and bloody, ragged, humiliated, his hands and elbows wired behind him, his feet wired so he could take eight-inch steps. From time-to-time the gook leading him on the rope would jerk the prisoner down and VC agitators among the villagers would shove people out to spit on the man, throw garbage on him, excrement, even make him lie on his back while some woman was made to squat over him and urinate in his face . . . unless, of course, they did not want to bother with the American, and simply shot him in the back and left him beside the trail.

By the time he landed, Brown wished he'd done it, wished he killed the man and his three captors. For the rest of them, the war was supposed to be winding down, but if that captured gunner lived, he might spend the next ten, fifteen, twenty-five years like an animal in a god damn zoo, on exhibit, a scrawny white man in rags, belly swollen with malnutrition, ribs showing; an example of how the peoples' republic had defeated the imperialistic aggressors . . . one poor son of a bitch who probably would some day be on his knees begging. But on the other hand he might just be another Rowe, the Special Forces officer from McAllen, Texas, they held prisoner and put on exhibit for six years, and tried to break down and bring over, and he finally beat them, and escaped from them, and got out.

They flew all day.

They lost another ship the fourth mission but got all the crew out. It was on the edge of the main fight, so with gunship and jet fighter-bomber protection, they also got a huge Skycrane helicopter into the site and lifted the Hog out and saved it, too.

Paseman and his crew kept up, making repairs and replacements, but toward dark, the Downhill Gang began running out of men. Doctor Holder and his medics treated the wounded and injured, and some of them Holder refused to certify for return to flight status. Brown did not say a word in protest, and Walker charged him, "What the fuck is going on here?"

"He's the doctor."

"He's an asshole."

"Better be careful, Captain; he's also a Major."

"He can ram that gold leaf up his bum. There's not a damned thing wrong with Webster but a little fragment through the palm of his hand. Shit, he's had worse cuts'n that opening beer cans!"

"He's the doctor."

"What the hell's happened to you? Why in the name of Christ did you get rid of Elmore?"

"Take it easy."

Brown said it mildly enough, but Walker must have seen he'd taken it as far as Brown intended for it to go, because he turned and walked away and finally rounded up another gunner to replace the grounded Webster. When the chime rang again an hour after dark, Walker's was the first ship into the air, then fell in as tail-end Charlie, the most dangerous position, where he always flew. Even so, he was only the fifth ship in the flight. There was an equal number of Hogs sitting useless on the ground back at base, because they could not be crewed.

On this gunship mission, another 504 Hog went in, all the way, the way they go in when the pilot gets shot through the face and the aircraft simply falls out of the sky, because there is no one flying it. The Hog went over on its back fifty feet in the air and then straight down. In the flares that lit the night sky on the mission, Brown saw one of the door-gunners dive out his side hatch in a desperate effort to make some attempt to save himself;

but it was the same thing as jumping off a three-story building afire and no men with the catch-net standing below.

The next time 504 scrambled, the Downhill Gang put two Hogs into the air, Brown and Walker. Both ships returned to base damaged, but with no wounded men. Ten minutes after Brown landed, Paulson called from Saigon. "What the hell's going on down there, Brown?"

"I'll play your stupid little riddle with you, General. What the hell's going on down here?"

"God damn you, if you've got some idea you're immune to discipline just because you've got a lot of fruit-salad on your chest and a big reputation, forget it. Until I'm transferred, I'm your commander; so knock off the smartass and answer me."

"What do you want to know?" Brown noticed Paulson had not said as soon as he was relieved; he had said transferred. . . .

"I've been getting the action reports all day, from all units engaged in this Quang Tri attack, and it's pretty god damn obvious that you've been putting fewer and fewer aircraft into the air each mission. This last one only two. Don't tell me you've run out of spares again."

"I've run out of men."

"All right, now, Brown, what the hell is this? I also have the casualty reports here on my desk."

"I've got a hardnosed flight surgeon."

"God damn it, who's running that outfit? You or the flight surgeon?"

"I am, but you know the regulations as well as I do. The flight surgeon has the last word on a man's fitness to fly. He can ground *you*, or the chief of army aviation, or Senator Barry Goldwater, if in his judgment he believes the man unfit to fly."

"What are you trying to pull?"

"I don't believe I understand the question, General."

"In a pig's— All right, here's an order: The 504th is to stand down until further orders, pending a board of inquiry."

"Inquiry into what, sir?"

"You'll be advised of that in due course."

"Am I relieved of command, General?"

"I'll let you know when I decide about that."

"Shall I get packed, just so there won't be any waste of time in case you do decide to relieve me?"

"Stop needling me, Brown. You have your orders. See that you follow them, exactly."

With precision, Brown anticipated the next move. While he had been on the telephone talking to General Paulson, Colonel March was already in the air in a Twin Bonanza enroute to 504's base. Fugate's intelligence network had warned him, and he came into Brown's office just minutes after Brown finished the telephone call. Brown listened to the information and said, "I figured that one. Just advise Holder. It's all we can do."

Brown looked up at Fugate from where he sat at his desk. "Frank, if you want out now, get out; it's the time to go. The building's falling down around us."

"I'm not worried. I was in intelligence work too long not to know intrigue and deception when I see it. I've covered my tracks and left myself about six escape routes. I hate like hell, though, to see you go under without a fight."

"I'm still fighting. It's just a different war. I guess I finally caught on, and I really don't feel very well about it."

March landed ten minutes later. He came off the airplane like a fighter-jockey who'd just scored the fifth victory that made him an Ace. He had assumed a strictly formal and severe attitude; he did not offer to shake hands.

After a brief conference in Brown's office, which March attempted to turn into an interrogation, Brown clamped down on him. "If this is an official investigation, then show me some papers, March; advise me of my rights, let me get the legal officer over here."

That took all the chest-out steam from March. He

158

tried the reverse pitch, "Aw, hell, Joe; you know the only reason I'm here is because Paulson sent me."

"Yeah, sure. And I bet you hated like hell to come down here tonight, too, didn't you?"

"Well, let's get on with it. What's the deal?"

"Exactly as I told Paulson. We've run out of men."

"Joe, I don't think this is any time for jokes. You may be up to your ass in alligators, whether you know it or not, acknowledge it or not."

"How does it feel?"

Deliberately, March lit a cigarette and blew smoke as he said, "I wouldn't know."

"No?"

"In case you hadn't heard, Joe, the two-star man took a good look at all that so-called evidence you put down before him; and once he had time to actually evaluate it, he put it where it belonged . . . in the shitcan." March smiled, blowing smoke, "He gave the kid a reprimand for inefficiency and transferred him. Make you happy?" March grinned again. "Hell, the kid didn't really want an army career anyway; he just had some pressure from me. He's damned near a scratch golfer and I'll line him up some sponsors and have him on the pro tour in a year."

Brown just held on. He wanted to kill the smirking man sitting before him, blowing smoke through his words as he talked, but Joe held on, not knowing how much longer he *could* have held on if March had kept twisting the knife. But the telephone rang and it may have saved Joe Brown from the charge of assault with intent. . . .

Brown answered, listened, acknowledged, hung up. To March he said, "The place for your inquiry is not in this office, but at the base hospital. Shall we go?"

Probably March saw the killer rising up in those green eyes, because the smirk went off his face and he rose immediately from his chair and went out the door. They walked in silence. Doctor Holder met them at the door. He conducted March through the wards, stopping at each airman's bed, taking up the chart hanging on a hook at the foot of the bed, reading off the nature and seriousness

159

of the wound or injury, the surgery or other care given each patient and the medication. Each time March protested that the wound or injury was ridiculously minor, Doctor Holder quoted directly from the flight surgeon's manual he carried in the pocket of his smock; in most cases, of course, involving mild wounds or injuries the cause for grounding the man was the medication he'd been given. Purely and simply, it was a matter of the various drugs containing some ingredient that had side effects similar to those of antihistamines, or alcoholic beverages. The regulation was absolute, providing no exceptions, even for wartime conditions: after taking a single dosage of such medications, either by injection or orally, an airman was automatically grounded, for no less than twelve consecutive hours. Each subsequent ingestion of the medication added another twelve hours to the mandatory grounding.

Brown knew as well as March knew; as well as the men in the beds knew; as well as Holder himself knew, that the regulation was knowingly and continuously violated in combat situations. In some outfits, in fact, after a man had been given medication that was a "downer"— likely to make him drowsy or affect his judgment or depth-perception—the flight surgeon had a ready supply of "uppers" which would alert and refresh the man so he could, and did, fly his missions. Doc Elmore had been such an FS, and for that reason he'd been chosen with care by Joe Brown. Doctor Holder represented a man of precisely the opposite philosophy, and he too had been chosen with equal care by Joe Brown.

Because Joe Brown had decided that he was not going to let the sons-of-bitching, incest-practicing, combination of news media people, rear-echelon military and politicians kill any more of his men. Joe Brown did no longer particularly think of the VC and the NVA as the *enemy*. They were people who shot at you when you went on missions, so you shot back; you tried to kill them before they killed you and your men. All the time, you knew you wouldn't even be shooting at one another if the

160

incesters would stop holding on for that last Big Chance to make a Big Reputation before the final pullout and they all went home.

It was make it here and now and make it Big, or you ended up as a network researcher instead of in front of the camera on the Evening News. You made it here and now, the graft, corruption, the kickbacks and payoffs stashed in Swiss bank accounts, or you went home with that sick feeling of how well you'd be now if you'd just had sense enough to get out of the game before that last big pot. You made it here and now or you missed your chance. Around the officers' clubs you knew deep down in the hurting place that you'd be assigned to command some ammunition depot, until the next list came out and you'd been passed over and you were out on your ass, selling real estate or insurance; or teaching high school math to make the difference between what it cost to live and how much of it the retirement check covered.

None of these rotten sons of bitches were kidding Joe Brown; especially the politicians, with their crappy catch phrases and fashionable jargon, using the POWs as pawns in Vietnam, the same way they did the blacks and the Latinos and the Indians back home. Words. Manure. Not an honorable motive among the whole lying shitass bunch of them. . . .

God damn, old Papa Hemingway had understood it a long time ago and put it down on paper; but none of the sons of bitches could read, apparently. Maybe because it was in such good straight English and not wrapped in public relations bullshit and ad-agency argot.

We have identified you, thought Joe Brown, looking at March, and seeing in him all the others he personified. You are the same breed, the incestuously-inbred common trash that we, somehow, through indifference or laziness or being too busy making a living and raising families, let get in command of us, and then kill us off. Well, Joe Brown thought, looking at March, no more of it for me. I read old Papa and know I know why Fred Henry did what he did: made the separate peace. Brown felt tears in

161

his eyes and he did not care, as he thought, I will not let you kill any more of my men.

They were in Paulson's private quarters, March's blouse off and tie drawn down from unfastened collar. A half-full bottle rested on the table between himself and General Paulson, who wore silk pajamas, robe and a pair of custom-made slippers. Paulson yawned, but he did not resent the 0300 hours intrusion; he'd given March orders to report in person, regardless of what time he returned from 504. Paulson gestured toward the bottle and March said, "Thanks," as he refilled his glass.

"You're convinced it's deliberate?" Paulson asked.

"Beyond any question."

"Then we've got him by the balls."

"Begging your pardon, general, but we do not—say again—we do not have him by the balls."

"But you said—"

"The whole problem is the flight surgeon, as I've tried to explain. He quoted me chapter and verse, just as I've told you."

Paulson slacked back in his chair for a moment. He shrugged, "Then get rid of him."

"We have no justification whatever for relieving Major Holder of his command. And if I may be permitted, we've had just about all the god damn heat we can take for monkeying with 504." March took a large swallow of his whisky, and sweat ran clammy and cold down his sides as he recalled the conference with the two-star man. That was not quite an accurate description of the meeting. March had not known that a man's voice could scald the hide off a man's ass, but that is exactly the sensation he felt after the two-star man let him go—raw and tender all about the lower parts of his body. And the two-star man had made it perfectly clear that the only reason he was not going through with it, all the way, and would not see March's hide hung out to dry was because, with the war drawing to a close, the news people were absolutely frantic for one final, huge scandal to make the army look

162

bad. Something that could go on and on and on, endlessly, like that god damn My Lai thing; for that reason the two-star man said, he was dropping it back to his "under advisement" file instead of at the top of his priority list. Sick, utterly sick and hollow, but having to know, March asked if he were through, his career ended. The two-star man smiled and said, "Colonel March, I'm sure a man as clever and resourceful as yourself will find a place into which you can fit perfectly."

Leaving the general's office, March had the uncomfortable sensation that what the two-star man meant was that March would find some superior officer's ass to stick his nose up, post-Paulson. . . .

"Hell, use your head, March," Paulson said. "Guys like this Holder are born specialists, the precision, detail types. Find out what his specialty is and where they need one Stateside, and transfer him, emergency. Then get someone like that Elmore back in there. Not Elmore himself, he and Brown are too good friends. Find some drunk who'll sign off any warm body that walks slowly past the door."

March took a drink and grinned, and said, "I know just the man."

"Then get it on, tonight. And make damned sure that 504 lacks nothing. I want a ton of extra spares, extra chow, *everything*, stacked around that outfit like it was a storehouse instead of an operational gunship base. Then, by God let's see that—that *bastard* cut his own throat."

March figured now was the time. He poured out another hooker of the general's excellent whisky, drank deeply, lit one of the general's cigars without first asking permission, and then March said, "And what do I get out of all this?"

Paulson simply looked at him, and March watched the silk-clad general closely. For a moment, Paulson seemed about to go into his Curt LeMay act, and then he said, "That's a rather stupid question, Colonel. You are a subordinate officer following orders. That's all. Now get out of here and get on with it."

March shook his head, puffed deeply on the illegal pure

163

Havana cigar, blew a ring toward the ceiling, and said, "What I am is a co-conspirator in the ruination of an outstanding career army officer."

Paulson reared up in his chair and March held up his hand. "Don't go off at half-cock, General; but let's don't be giving *me* any of the LeMay act. I've put my ass and my whole career, my life, on the line for you; and, General Paulson, I do not contribute those professional services free of charge to *anyone!*"

For a moment Paulson stared at March, then said, "I could break you in a moment, March; in ten seconds."

"And I'd drag you right down into the shit with me, neck deep; then pull you under and watch you drown. I'm not afraid of you, and have never been. I'm army, as you are, and I go army, the way it's shaped up out here, now. If it doesn't sicken you, then you're less a man than I think, because it sickens me and I don't gag easy. But I never got to eagle colonel without learning to ride with the punches, without doing what has to be done, as nasty as the doing is sometimes." With a snort of contempt, March threw the cigar on the floor, and said, "The army isn't running this war out here now, nor the navy; and all the Marines have been pulled out. It's all politics. It's come down to a simple matter of make it while it lasts."

Paulson nodded once, abruptly, in complete agreement.

March said, "I want the 504th. I want it now, tonight. I want to be the last commander of the hottest, most publicized gunship unit in the army. I'll grow a handlebar mustache, wear a weird hardhat or fly mission in a jockstrap, whatever it takes. All you have to do is see to it that those media people have cause to be out there, almost every day, sound-on-film cameras ready."

"And just how the hell do you expect to arrange all that?" Paulson reached for one of his cigars and jammed it into his mouth, chomping down. "You reminded me, yourself, as though I needed it for God's sake, *who* and *what* Joe Brown is, not only by reputation but for real!"

March reached for his blouse, flipped it back, and took a folded paper from the inside pocket. He unfolded it and handed it to Paulson. Paulson took his reading glasses from the pocket of his robe and read, twice looking up at March, then read on to the end.

"Where did you get this?"

"The only thing that matters is that I can verify its authenticity, absolutely. Incidentally, the man who signed it is 504's new flight surgeon. He's flying in from Melbourne tonight."

"It puts the crunch on him, all right." Paulson chomped his cigar as March watched him, thoughtfully. "All right," Paulson said, "It's all yours, just as you put it, except your timing's wrong. You're too damned eager."

"How's that?"

"Christ, March, your ambition is completely destroying your judgment." Paulson peeled a string of tobacco from inside his mouth and wadded it into an ashtray. "Get Holder out and replace him with Christensen—and you'd better be damned sure Christensen is the tame FS you claim—then let them fight it out for a few days. I think it will come to this: Christensen will certify men that Brown wants to keep grounded. Brown will overrule and you'll have Christensen file the proper report, that, in his judgment, Brown is deliberately controverting Christensen's certifications of men for flight status; to the detriment of the war effort."

"Then you land on him and I take over."

"Precisely. You, ah, can wait a week, can't you?"

"To cut that redskin son of a bitch's strings and ruin him, I could wait a year."

Paulson laughed, and said, "I've waited almost twenty-five years."

Astonished, but honestly delighted, Holder accepted his transfer orders with a sort of numbness. An emergency transfer to Brooks Army Medical Center, in San Antonio, Texas, where an expert opthalmologist was required immediately. With unconcealed happiness, he packed and departed in two hours time, going out on the same Blue Canoe that brought Major Christensen to 504 as Holder's replacement.

Christensen's interview with Brown was not friendly; even when Joe tried to joke away what the doctor had done to him with those tranquilizers when Joe was on R&R in Melbourne with his wife. After the interview was concluded, Joe sat back and thought about it. He had the distinct feeling he'd just been talking to a man who knew something that Joe Brown did not, a man who held an edge over Joe Brown, despite the fact Brown was two full ranks higher and commander of the unit to which this pink-faced son of a bitch had just reported. Christensen had exactly the opposite attitude from what a commanding officer had every right to expect of a new arrival.

Fifteen minutes later, Joe Brown learned why.

Fugate came into the office, carrying a coffeepot and two cups. While he poured with one hand, he took a folded piece of paper from his pocket and handed it to Joe Brown. Joe read it, with astonishment; when he looked up Fugate said in his usual, mild voice, "Any questions as to why we have a new flight surgeon; and why he just happens to be this particular man?"

"This is— You had this the day we saw the general?"

"I did. Perhaps I made a mistake not showing it that day; but the way it's all turned, I think it would have gone into the same dead file as the other, obviously, has gone."

"It doesn't matter, Frank. I just want you to do one more thing for me."

"Anything."

"Get out. Write yourself some orders and I'll endorse them."

"I won't quit you, Joe."

"I know that; it's why I'm telling you go haul your ass out of here. You know what this set up is. Christensen is going to certify men for flight that I don't want in the air, because I don't want them killed. If you stick, it means you back me. You'd just as well be trying to ride a dead horse. What aircraft are you not current in?"

Fugate reluctantly named several helicopters and one fixed-wing, single-engine airplane. Brown asked, "Are you current on your instrument rating?"

"No." Again reluctantly.

"Cut yourself orders for flight proficiency checkrides. Bring them to me in ten minutes. I know how fast you type. I'll endorse your orders, and I want you off this base within the hour."

"Joe, I can't quit you."

"You're not quitting, you're a lousy pilot who's not current and can't fly missions and I'm shaping you up." They both grinned and Fugate left. He came back in seven minutes with the orders; Joe Brown signed them and they shook hands. Fugate left; Brown stood in the door of his office until he saw the Blue Canoe lift off; then, he went to challenge Major Christensen.

He found Christensen going through the files, before making a round of the wards. Without, personally, examining the men he was putting the medical records into two stacks; those which he intended, still without personal examination, to return to flight status and those he simply dared not.

Brown closed the door behind him and leaned against it. He asked Christensen, "How would you like to say the lies, to my face, that you wrote in your report?"

Brown figured the reason Christensen did not answer. He was probably trying to figure if he could—with safety and chance of survival—dive through the window of his office and escape this vast dark-complexioned green-eyed, lefthanded man, who appeared totally consumed with anger; to the point that the threat of courts-martial, jail or even death could not stop him from doing what he had in mind to do.

But it never really came to that.

Brown simply told him, "Don't do it. Do you understand me, Doctor Christensen? Don't do it. The men who are grounded are to remain grounded, so long as I am in command of this base, of this unit, of 504, the Downhill Gang. Do you understand?"

"Sir, my job is—"

"No, you are not answering my question. Do you understand the order I have given you?"

"Yes, sir, but I—"

"Can you type?"

"Of course."

"Then roll in an original, as many carbons as you think you'll need and write this." Brown gave the doctor time to get his papers prepared, with rattling hands. Then, slowly, a word at a time he dictated the memo, feeling the noose draw tighter and tighter around his neck as he dictated. When the doctor finished, Brown stepped across the room, drew the papers from the machine and signed each copy with his back-slanted, lefthanded signature. He did not scribble; he made his name large and completely legible.

He folded one copy, put it into his pocket, and said, "Now, you baboonass-faced creep, get on the horn to your pals in Saigon; March, Paulson and whoever else. Tell them what I have done. March should be packed and ready. You'll make a fine threesome, you will; you running along behind March with your mouth stuck to his butt, while he's got his nose up Paulson's ass."

Brown sat down on the edge of Christensen's desk. "Just keep one thing in mind. Until I am officially relieved of my command here, I am in command. Send one man into the air, just *one*, and your ass is *mine!*"

As he walked back toward his office, the klaxon *ooogaah* shattered the air. Brown ran for his ship and flew the last gunship mission he was ever to fly.

Two ships. Brown and the faithful Walker.

Both ships returned, shot to pieces. Walker made a miraculous landing, because he was one of the winners; he just wanted it that bad. But his facial, shoulder and stomach wounds were so severe that Christensen and his medics could only do the obvious, then a Dustoff—a casualty evacuation helicopter—came in and flew him out to the big hospital. One of Walker's crewmen was dead, the other unharmed, physically. Except he stepped off the gunship with the wide, vacant, staring eyes of a round-the-bend psycho; and medics had to lead him by the hand

168

to the hospital where Christensen, who seemed to be catching on, gave the door-gunner a massive sedative.

Brown had a wound, the kind the old western pulps called a "graze" across his face; and a splinter of plastic windshield in his neck that a medic plucked out with a pair of tweezers. Both his door-gunners were unhit, and March waited on the ramp. Brown led the way to his office; when March began the stupid, inane little change-of-command formalities, Brown simply grabbed him with his left hand by the throat and banged March against the wall. He held him there until the beautiful, capped teeth began to show a bulge of blackening tongue between them and the movie-star blue eyes bulged almost outside their sockets. Brown watched March; when the eyes began to drift, go erratic, cross and wander and the man was almost as much dead as he was alive, then, Brown released him and let him fall to the floor.

Brown went over to his desk, picked up the pot of cold coffee, and, from the spout, he poured watery, cold glop into March's left ear until the man began to moan and move and bat his hand at the annoyance. Brown went back to the desk, sat with one hip cocked up on it and watched March come around. After a few minutes, March righted himself with his back against the wall, legs spread, breathing deeply, shudderingly. He looked very unlike March, the polished, tailored, gleaming, photogenically statuesque eagle colonel of the United States Army (Aviation). He looked, instead, like a pile of soggy rags with a man somewhere inside them who was not too certain where he was; or what, or, precisely who!

Brown let March find the handles to reality, get his eyes focused, and make sure his knees would bend; that he was truly among the survivors. Then, Brown stepped over to him and slapped March's face, open-handed, as hard as he could. It very quickly got the colonel's attention. Brown went back to the desk and hiked his hip upon it, watching March's eyes clear and his whole posture become aware and alert.

Brown said, "Get on your feet, March."

March came up like a toy on springs and stood leaning against the wall. Brown didn't move, except to look at the man, face-to-feet and back again. Brown said, "It is all yours, colonel. Everything. But I have not decided exactly when I'll leave yet, certainly not before the Blue Canoe returns from carrying out Lieutenant Colonel Fugate."

Just as a test, Brown moved suddenly, and March flinched, so Brown knew he had the man under control. "You stay here, March, in this office. I'll have a pot of coffee and some brandy sent in for you. Rest. Look through the paper work. Decide upon who'll be your adjutant. Familiarize yourself. But don't leave this office before I return."

Brown lunged at March and the pitiful son of a bitch cowered away, covering his head with his arms. Brown went out and left him there. He found Charles, several other gunners and five or six pilots, CWO Webb and others; and they went over to the maintenance shops, got cans of black spray paint; and, in an hour, they obliterated every last vestige of the Downhill Gang. The brand on the gunships, the signs in the officers' club and the EM club; on walls and hangar doors, so that when Joe Brown finished and shook hands with the men who'd helped him, it might have been that no such thing had ever existed. As he walked back to his office, and told the new clerk, Louderback, to get all the personal gear ready, the Blue Canoe landed. Brown went by communications center and told the duty operator to have the Cessna refueled and ready to leave at once. He went to his room, got his small amount of gear, told the new clerk to load it aboard the airplane, went back to the office and went in without knocking.

March was on the telephone, talking desperately. He jerked with fear and surprise at Brown's entry. Brown indicated the telephone. "Paulson?"

March nodded.

Brown took the telephone. "OK, Little LeMay, it's all

your boy's command now. I've got my orders and I'm checking out. If you want me, I'll be in Arizona."

"You report directly to me or I'll have you arrested."

"Do you really think that the only copies of those papers we had were the ones we turned over to the two-star man? When I hang up, I'm going aboard my Cessna direct to Tan Son Nhut. Have someone meet me there with endorsements for my orders. Word them any way you wish. Relieved of command. Psycho. Posted to inactive duty. On leave without pay. Subject to military inquiry. Just so long as I have orders. Don't even consider any kind of AWOL horseshit, or I'll land in your lap like a ton of scrap iron."

Brown hung up and went out without looking at March.

15

As the C-151 turned on downwind to land at Andrews
Air Force Base near Washington, D.C., one of the crewmen went back to wake Colonel Brown. The crewman
stood for a moment, looking down at the man; he shook
his head. The crewman had flown many missions to and
from Vietnam, taking the fresh ones out, bringing the
used-up men home; and he had never seen a whole man
so wasted as this colonel. He had seen worse-looking men
—the maimed and blind and psycho cases the flight
nurses kept so heavily sedated they hardly moved, and
who were, even then, strapped down to the litters on
which they lay.

But this man's hollowed cheeks, his restlessly fluttering
eyelids, the big, bony hands and wrists, the way his collar
looked three sizes too large! The crewman thought, he
must be forty, fifty pounds under his normal weight.

The airman reached out and touched Brown's shoulder.
Joe Brown came instantly awake, eyes sprung so wide
and staring the crewman thought, they look like two urine
holes in a dirty snowbank.

"Buckle up, sir; we're landing."

Brown nodded and fastened the seat belt. He sat up
and looked over his shoulder and saw that his guard was
still with him. Of course the man had not been overt or
declared his assignment, but Joe Brown caught on to him
about ten minutes after the man had come into view at
Tan Son Nhut. After that, he was there everytime Brown
looked up, even at the next urinal when he went to the
latrine, when they landed in Hawaii to refuel. Brown
finished up and zippered his trousers and told the man,
"If it would help, why not just handcuff yourself to me?"

The man, a major in the uniform of an infantry regiment, flushed deeply and turned his head away. Brown persisted, "Doesn't it make you feel a little crappy, a CID hotshot wearing a fighting man's insignia?"

Still the man didn't answer. He kept his head down as though he could not attend to his business without watching it happen. Deliberately Brown reached out and shoved the man's right elbow.

The CID man jumped sideways, too late; the stain on his trousers. Deeply angered, he turned to face Brown, and smiling widely, Joe said, "Gee, feller, I *am* sorry." Then he walked out fast, but once the door to the latrine closed, Joe stood directly in front of it, so when the CID man rushed out he almost ran over Brown. He mumbled something and started around Brown, but Joe cut him off, and stepped close, then closer, backing the man against the wall. "Stay out of my sight. I mean if you've got a job, keeping me in view, to make sure I don't take off on you, fine. But put the tail back behind, near the asshole, where you belong."

The major started to say something. Brown told him, "None of that crap about how a CID man on a case outranks everyone. Unless you place me under arrest, then keep your place, behind and to the left."

There had not been any further harassment after that; except that Joe had seen the CID man show the aircrew some papers as they boarded the C-151, probably telling them to help him keep an eye on the crazy colonel, because he couldn't hope to stay awake all the way to Washington.

Brown figured it must have spoiled the CID man's entire day, if not his whole trip, when the pilot and co-pilot handed the papers back to the CID man, left him standing with the enlisted flight personnel, came over to introduce themselves and shake Joe Brown's hand.

But that was all behind. Ahead, Joe Brown anticipated the crunch. He knew how sick he was of flying when he did not, automatically, "help the pilot land" the airplane at Andrews. At the foot of the ramp, a lieutenant colonel stepped forward and saluted Brown. Absently, almost contemptuously, Brown flicked a vague return salute; he was looking at the crossed-flintlock pistols insignia on the light colonel's tunic lapels. Brown didn't catch the man's name, and he acted as though he did not see the hand the man offered to shake. He asked simply, "Am I under arrest?"

"Of course not, Colonel." The MP officer acted as though this were the most outrageous question he'd ever heard.

"You're just taking over for this clown, are you?" Brown jerked his left hand at the major who'd accompanied him halfway across the world. Before the MP officer could answer, Joe leaned forward and in a loud stage whisper said, "You'd better get him in to see the medics. He pees his pants." Joe paused, then: "I *saw* him do it!"

For a moment, there was a stunned silence, then Brown said in a voice that made the words sound like breaking sticks, "Get someone to secure my gear and let's go." He shoved past the MP officer, who had to run to catch up. "Over here, Colonel Brown. We have a car."

On the drive into town, all the whole, long way to the Pentagon, neither man spoke a word and the driver never once craned his neck to get a look at Brown in the rearview mirror. At the vast building the driver drew to a smooth stop before one of the entrances, bailed out, ran around the car and opened the door, saluting, as Brown followed the MP officer out of the back seat.

"Shall I wait, sir?" asked the driver.

"Yes, I'll only be a moment."

"Soon as he's delivered the prisoner," Brown said.

The MP officer's head snapped around and he stared at Brown; but he could not face the coyotelike stare of Joe's green, yellowish-tinged eyes. He ducked his head and said, "If you will follow me, please?"

"Mind your manners, Colonel," Joe Brown snapped.

174

The MP halted instantly, faced Brown and came to attention. "Sir? . . ."

"You said I was not under arrest."

"That is correct, Colonel Brown."

"We are going to General Randolph's office."

"Correct, sir."

"Then you get where you belong according to proper military courtesy and discipline. Until one thing or another happens to alter our present relationship, then you will walk on my left, and preferably about one-half step behind. I know the way to General Randolph's office. I have been there before."

The MP officer's face went dead white. Probably never before in his life, certainly not in his military career, had he been spoken to in quite that tone of voice, with the impact of suppressed violence and absolute authority. Certainly not before witnesses, of which there were many —officers and enlisted men, civilians, his own driver. At least fifteen people had stopped, gawking, at the sound of that scrapiron voice. Cruelly, because of his complete anger, Brown let the MP soak in it a moment; then, he strode past the white-faced officer, went up the steps and into the vast building.

They did not say another word to one another. The MP opened the door to General Randolph's outer office and Brown went inside. The enlisted clerk, a recruiting poster WAC tech sergeant, leaped to her feet, as did the 1/Lt. wearing staff shields on his tunic. Both snapped perfect salutes, then, the lieutenant stepped forward and spoke to the MP officer, "Thank you, Colonel. The general said you need not wait."

The MP nodded and started to back out the door, when Brown went up the side of his head again. "You need a lesson in manners. Haven't you forgotten something? Are you not supposed to ask the senior officer present for permission to leave his presence?"

The MP lieutenant colonel's hand shook as he saluted rigidly, and his voice cracked: "By your leave, sir?"

Brown looked him over for a moment, then stepped

close and said softly, "I'm hoping the same thing you are, that we meet again some day." Brown stepped back, snapped a return salute and said, "Dismissed."

The MP virtually ran from the room.

Brown faced the room again. The WAC's face looked as though it had been covered with dead-white chalk. The lieutenant followed the rule: "When in doubt, salute."

He snapped off another, then said, "The chief of staff is expecting you, sir. Go right in." He indicated a door.

"Thank you," Joe Brown said. He removed his cap, went to the door, knocked three times and went inside.

Brigadier General Wallace looked up from under deliberately-cultivated, bushy, thick eyebrows, like Admiral Halsey had 'way back then.' For a moment, the two men simply regarded one another, almost like two strange horses suddenly put into the same waterlot, snuffling and watching, presenting themselves to one another. Then, Brown stepped across the room and reported in proper military fashion. Wallace returned the salute and gestured toward a chair near the left corner of his desk. "Sit down, Colonel."

Joe Brown remained standing, his coyotelike gaze fastened on Wallace's face. He saw the red flush rise in Wallace's neck and inflame his ears. Very distinctly, Brown said, "I'll take whatever you people have planned for me, General. But I'll only take it once."

Wallace lurched to his feet, Office work, flying the chair, had not been good for Wallace; he was as much over his healthy weight as Brown was under his own.

"Colonel, that is an order. *Sit down!*"

Brown did not move. He regarded Wallace, pointedly looking at the vast belly that the best tailor of uniforms in Washington had not been able to reduce, much less hide. Brown said, "I'll take *one* raking over, from The Man. Then we can get on with whatever charges and specifications you people have got in mind. But if you think, for a second, that I'm going to sit still for one reaming after another all the way up the line; have every chickenshit, chairborne mastermind in this building who

176

outranks me stuff barbed wire up my ass and pull it out while I squirm, you can forget it."

Wallace leaned forward, peering at Brown with astonishment, and after a moment he said, "By God, I think they just might be right. You *have* lost your god damn mind!"

Sudden tears sprang to Joe Brown's eyes and he could not help them. After he clamped his teeth and swallowed, he leaned forward and shouted into Wallace's face. "The only thing I lost was a lot of *men*, for no god damn reason at all, except to make fat slobass politicians like you look good sitting behind your desks, totaling up the fucking *body count*; then, sending out a medal for a butchering son of a bitch like March. For making a record! The most gunship missions flown in a single twenty-four-hour period in the whole nine years of the War! There's just one thing some son of a bitch overlooked. March kept the average—he got at least one of *my* men killed for every one of those missions, and not even I know how many of *my* men lost eyes, and arms, or had their balls shot off and—"

Brown was abruptly aware that a door to his left had opened and he shot a look at it. General Pate Randolph stood there, grim and unreadable. The silence in the room was as deep and profound as a night alone at sea in a life raft, and almost as spooky.

For at least a half-minute, not one of the three men moved; none spoke, the only sound—after a while—was Wallace's panting breath.

In a dry, crisply crackling voice, General Pate Randolph said, "Come in, Colonel."

Wallace recovered enough to gulp, "Sir, I demand—"

The door of Randolph's office closed in his face as Brown entered and the general swung the door shut. Randolph gestured toward a chair and, gratefully, Brown sat down; he felt exhausted. He felt his too-large uniform bunching sweatily and uncomfortably and tried to squirm himself to a better position, anticipating a long session with the reamer.

General Randolph opened a cigar box on his desk and

pushed it toward Brown. Brown took one, bit off the end and put the wet tobacco in a huge ashtray while Randolph did the same. Each man lighted his own, and then Randolph said, "Joe, what are your plans?"

Totally astonished, Brown said, "My plans?"

"I just thought I'd inquire, sort of try to keep up. You seem to have developed a habit of doing things on your own, lately, and then, letting the rest of the army find out about them at your convenience."

"General, I'm here to face whatever charges and specifications you have ready. With your permission, I can get along entirely without the sarcasm."

Randolph's eyebrows shot up as though he were truly surprised. "Sarcasm?"

Brown leaned forward in his chair. "If you don't mind, let's stop the fencing, the semantics, the game. I'm tired; thirsty, worn out, homesick, hungry and I want to see my wife."

Joe paused, wiped sweat from his face, and in a sort of daze, looked around for somthing to dry his hand on; and, finally, pulled out a handkerchief and wiped his face again. All this while, Randolph sat back in his chair and puffed slowly on his cigar.

"I did what I did," Brown said. "I've got coming one—*one*—chewing out. Let's have it, and then get on with the rest of it."

"You sound like a quitter."

"If you're talking about the useless killing of my men, you've not stated it quite right. I don't *sound* like a quitter. I *quit*."

"That easy, that simple, that quick."

"Exactly." Brown sat back in his chair and looked at Randolph. Despite himself, Brown could not quite keep the sneering combat man's condescension for the rear echelon from his voice. "You should have gone along on a gunship mission or two, when you were out there on one of those *inspection trips*." Brown made it sound like exactly what he believed a general's inspection trip consisted of, which was the same as that of a congressman or

178

high-powered news media man: sampling discreetly the delights of the East . . . little Viet pussy, command performances by whatever USO show happened to be in Saigon, a look at the schoolhouses, hospitals and plumbing installed in a model village under the pacification program. Then, one fast ride in a gunship, escorted by a whole squadron of fully-ordnanced F4 *Phantom II*s, out to a firebase, and back; and step off the helicopter right into a cluster for the many-clustered Silver Star already on his chest.

Pate Randolph leaned forward and jammed out the fire of his cigar. His anger made red spots high on each cheek. "Don't give me any of that. What do you think I was doing in forty-three, forty-four and forty-five, while you were on your high school ass back home, trying to decide on accepting appointment to the Academy or go for one of the big scholarship offers with under-the-table-money for your boxing prowess? I was up to my chin in blood and guts and muddy slime fighting the infantry war. You keep talking *your* men, about them killing *your* men. The outfit I landed with on Utah Beach suffered *seven hundred* percent casualties from D-Day till Germany quit! I was never out of the lines more than six weeks the whole time. And where were you, and doing what, when Korea cracked wide open? Boxing. I was not only among the very first helicopter pilots sent to Korea, I was one of the very last to leave. And the only reason I stayed so long, hung in there, was that we had to *prove*, we had to *convince*, every son of a bitch from weekly newspaper editors to lobbyists—to congress and Truman himself—that the army still *had to have* its own aircraft. Instead of depending entirely upon the air force when they made the air force a separate entity. You bitch about doing five tours in Vietnam, and justly so. You know how many tours I did in Korea? One, that's all, one tour and it was damned near three years long! That's while you were boxing your last year and thinking about quitting the army. After deciding to stay in you went to flight school and managed a few—how many? Thirty, twenty-five?—missions in Korea, at the tail-end of the thing."

Brown nodded, and then he too leaned forward, speaking with equal flat, crackling bluntness. "So I was born too late to hit the beach on D-Day; but you've got a memory like a sieve, General. That's right, I flew a *few* missions in Korea, right at the tail-end of the war, when our side took more casualties than in the previous two-and-a-half years! Why don't you remember Carson, and Vegas, and Bunker and all the other god damn hills?"

"Don't quote names and places to me, son. You were a punkass lieutenant making trooplifts and evacuating wounded. I was not only flying those missions but, along with the Marines, was trying to make illegal airframe modifications to arm those naked sons-of-bitching-death-traps. At the same time I was fighting the other battle with politicians—and that's what I'm still doing, trying to keep what we have, trying to get more of what we need, project ten years ahead; fighting the air force and the navy and Marines for priorities, trying to convince stupid self-serving congressmen that we are not overlapping. That there is no duplication of effort or inefficient utilization because some Marine units or Special Forces outfits have the same kind of aircraft we fly. Trying, sometimes simply and clearly, begging kissass abominable people, even have the cretins into my *home* to make passes at my wife, so I can try to convince them that without the guns there will be no butter with an American brand name. Everytime I turn around, I find myself in position comparable to a doctor. By his skill, dedication, training and maximum effort, he performed the operation, but the patient thanks *God* for saving his life. That's how we are, in reverse, sent out to do men's jobs with children's tools and, sometimes, with nothing at all. Except the tough, lean, hard young men you mentioned, yourself. The kind of man *you* are. God damn it, I don't have to tell you what you did with that miserable 504th, do I?"

General Randolph banged his fists on his desk. "These lying sons of bitches shaft us from every direction; they

180

blame it *all* on us. You know as well as I do, and by God to use that man's words, so do the American people know in their hearts: that we could have won that war just as easily, just as quickly, as we won in Korea. In six months we knocked them back to the Yalu; it was over. Then the Chinese came in and oh, my goodness, get back, get out of there, we don't want a war with *China*! War with China, my ass! There would have been no war with China. This time, the same bunch got hold of the guerilla-warfare manure, that a conventional armed force simply could not beat a so-called people's army.

"We did. We pounded sand up their asses, until they made us stop; until the news media began practicing incest, just as you told Paulson, and every story that came out of Vietnam was deliberately slanted to make us look bad, not the fucking VC or Ho Chi Minh. And because of that, I will concede—hell, I admit—that plenty of what you told Paulson in Saigon is absolutely true. We do practice incest with the press, because if we don't, then we get it up the ass, wrapped in barbed wire with triple-handles. Look at that so-called Petagon Papers exposé and all the shit it spun off. These bastards shout about protecting the people's right to know, but what about protecting the people's right for the enemy *not* to know?"

Brown held up his hand. "All right, all right, I got the message. You've got a tough job. I don't envy you."

"No, you just want to quit me."

Randolph leaned back in his chair, biting off the end of another cigar. This time he did not bother to delicately put the string of tobacco in the ashtray. With obvious anger, he spat it on the thick carpet. "Like some damned kid who lost his marbles, you want to pack it in. If I can't win, I ain't gonna play."

Randolph leaned forward, elbows on his desk. "You know something? With your attitude now, you couldn't be on *my* boxing team. You'd take a Sunday on the nose that made your eyes water and you'd call for your mother."

"Shit!"

"Then explain what all this recent big behavior of yours has been all about."

"My God, how dumb do you have to be, how bad a mistake do you have to make, to be promoted to general?"

Randolph did nothing but light his cigar and blow smoke in Brown's face. Angrily Joe batted the murk away and said, "What the hell do you think it's all about? I refused to let them kill any more of my men."

"And accomplished precisely what?"

Brown looked at Randolph.

Randolph jabbed his cigar at Joe Brown. "Just this. You delivered your precious men into the hands of a god damn ambitious butcher. If you are any kind of man at all, you cannot sit there and blame March. You sit there and look inside that hollowed-out sinking feel in your guts and blame Joe Brown; because you walked out on them, you quit them, and now, you want to quit me."

"That's a god damn lie, and you know it is."

"How do you think it will look to a courts-martial?"

"Just as you said, I'm sure. But don't forget that I have a round in that fight, too."

"I see. Then, what your real motive in all this is is simply to drag the army down in the shit; and then, emerge some kind of spattered, bloody-but-unbowed hero. Then what? Going to write a book? Or maybe you've got some photos you'll sell to some magazine for fifty-thousand, like the My Lai person, *after* you achieve sufficient notoriety?" Randolph blew smoke again. "Of course you won't go to jail. A man with your record? Christ! So you've got it made, haven't you?"

Brown shook his head unable to believe that, after all these years and the personal closeness he had with Pate Randolph, the general could so completely misunderstand, misinterpret, Brown's motives. He put out his own cigar and moved forward in his chair. All he wanted to do now was get out. To hear the charges and specifications read to him, then, start arranging for an attorney and learning how to bull his way through slobbering packs of media people, saying "No comment!"

Randolph said, "I won't let you do it, Joe."

"Do what?"

"Quit me."

"God damn it, you keep saying that, using that expression. What the hell does it mean, what do you want from me?"

"To stick and fight."

"Fight what, for the sake of Christ?"

"All the lousy rotten things you've been blowing your loudmouthed stack about the past four days, which can be summed up in a single word: *expediency*. Remember that word. It is the throne at which politicians worship. I want you here with me, to help me, to make them learn, once and for all god damn time, that the end does *not* justify the means. That it is not *expedient*, for the moment, to let our POWs languish, and keep getting our men killed, or start new wars on false grounds in the future. I want you to stay with me and help fight this malicious, vicious, unrelenting propaganda directed at us. That we are trying to take over the country; that we all take kickbacks, rape babies, murder grandmothers, napalm pregnant women. That ninety percent of our men and half our officers have experimented with drugs; that —oh, hell! Joe, they'll *listen* to a man like you. They *have* to. Like they listened to David Shoup when he was Commandant of the Marine Corps. He was just too god damn much of a man to ignore, to turn that snotty tone loose on with insinuations and those god damn, 'Have you stopped beating your wife? Answer yes-or-no'-type questions."

Joe Brown did not know why he did not accept at once, because he knew he would. He'd love turning his guns on the oily-voiced, insinuating bastards who'd bought their ways in through rigged elections back home or rode in on the reputation of dead men. Or because it was their turn, having worked up through the party from ward heeler to representative; then, to senator, ruthlessly citing war records, memberships, work with the disadvantaged. Or sucking up to the youth vote, the black, the Mexican-

Americans, the Indian tribes; playing their little games of incest with the media, leaking what would hurt opponents, perjuring themselves to conceal their own conspiracies. . . .

"Joe? . . ."

"On one condition."

"Anything you say."

"Get the word around. I mean all around, so well that even the usual ten-percenters who seem never to get the word, do get *this* word. I'll trade these eagles for the stockade the first time one of those boozy bastards touches Jody, because I'll tear his fucking head off."

General Randolph rose and leaned across his desk, hand out. "Deal."

Joe Brown held the general's hand in a firm and friendly grip, and stared directly into his eyes. "I mean it, Pate. No matter which of them, where, when." Joe looked down at his left hand. "Seventeen is an odd number and I'd just as soon go for even and make it eighteen."

General Randolph nodded and as they released hands, he grinned and said, "So long as the subject's come up. . . ." Randolph picked up one of the several telephones on his desk, of various colors; this one happened to be black. He punched a button and, after a moment, said, "All right, sergeant."

A moment later, the recruiting-poster WAC sergeant opened the door, then, stepped aside and Jody came in.

Bestsellers by
William Crawford

THE CHINESE CONNECTION, by William Crawford. A novel of violence and suspense on the Mexican border. This is an absorbing tale of drug running and murder in the Southwest—with strange ties to the Far East. With a unique and richly conceived cast of characters, it reveals a world of which *The French Connection* offered a first hint. For these are people who would stop at nothing to attain their goals—for whom violence, sex, bribery and assassination are only way stations on the road to the big money, and to the power that money will buy. It's up to one honest man—a man not afraid to kill—to stop the scheme.
P232—95¢

THE MARINE, by William Crawford. A stirring novel of war, heroism, patriotism. It's Jim Garrison's story—a U.S. Marine and 100% American. However, this isn't a story of handsome men in fancy dress uniforms, or the spectacle of military parades . . . it's a gut-rending, realistic account of a man trying to survive a war. And he does make it, through the hell of it all—brutality, starvation, torture. Then Jim is hit with an even more grisly situation. He has to face trial for his action in a Vietnam POW camp! His court martial puts his life on the line, and we find that the trial is also a test of our military traditions and patriotism.
P126—95¢

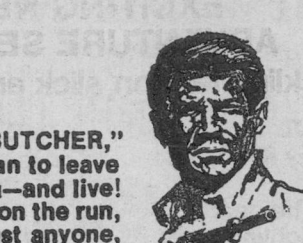

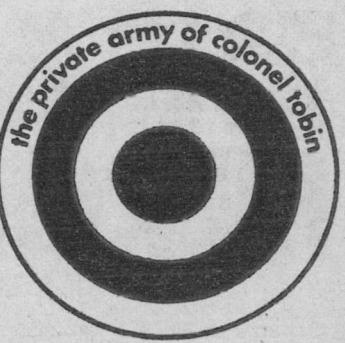